Secrets of the Water Meadow

Dawn Meredith

DEDICATION

To my family in Norway, for all the wonderful childhood
memories I treasure.

Other books by Dawn Meredith:

Junior fiction:
The Wobbly Wombat
The Anything Shop
Phantom Spies
Friend in a Shell
Fat Abby – Feline Investigator

Junior Non-fiction:
Sir Donald Bradman
The Boy Who Went to War
12 Annoying Monsters – Self Talk for Kids with Anxiety

Young Adult Fiction:
Rebel – book one of the FLIGHT trilogy
Elkwood
The Whispering Stone

Adult Fiction:
Letters from the Dead

ACKNOWLEDGMENTS

My deepest thanks go to my faithful test readers, but especially my cousins Heidi and Monica, for enjoying the story and characters so much. It has been a wonderful opportunity for reliving our shared childhood memories on Sekken. They also advised about Norwegian culture and language.

Names of places and people have been changed. Also, I designed a traditional bunad dress for Eikeberg island from my imagination. It does not represent any particular region of Norway. (dress outfits for men and women are very proudly region based and very specific).

I want to thank Lucinda Sharp from Forty South publishing for loving this story of a girl and her wild mermaid friend as much as I do. We live on the island of Tasmania and island life is definitely different to anything else! The wildness of nature is all around us. I see it every day on our 100 acre farm and feel so very lucky to live in this beautiful place.

CHAPTER ONE

It was five o'clock in the morning. A sour wind stirred the small, restless waves in jagged white lines towards the grey-pebbled shore of Eikeberg Island. Eleven year old Freya stood submerged to her calves in frigid sea water, her nightie clutched high, her long brown hair gently moving in the breeze. Her toes, scrunched on the uneven pebbles, were numb. Thick ribbons of knobbly yellow seaweed slithered round her legs in the swirling water, sending goose bumps right up to her face. But Freya dared not move. If she stood perfectly still, and made no sound, she might see the beautiful *havfrue*, (mermaid), called Lorelei. Five o'clock was the exact time her elder sister Lisbet insisted the havfrue came to feed in the shallows. And Freya didn't want to miss it.

A pale pink horizon graced the snowy peaks on the opposite side of the fjord with a shimmering lustre, like pink icing on a cake. In a shallow valley at the shoreline sat the small Norwegian town of Stranda. If she squinted, Freya could see a fishing boat making its way from the harbour for the fishing grounds further up Strandafjord and out of sight. On a slope just behind Freya stood her ancestral home, Fjellheim, (mountain home) a sleepy, white painted wooden house, with her tiny attic bedroom facing the fjord. An impressive barn of great slabs of rough-sawn oak painted red with white trim stood beside the house, where it had been for over three hundred years. But that was not nearly as long as the merfolk had inhabited the deep of Strandafjord.

Legend called them *mørke engler*, (dark angels), to be feared and distrusted. Freya's mother, German by birth, called them Lorelei. Only the old ones, like their elderly neighbour Gamle Jenny, (old jenny) believed the mørke engler actually existed, but folk legend had created strict rules, especially for children. On Eikeberg Island small children were never allowed to bathe alone or even stand in the fjord waters without supervision. But Lisbet insisted Lorelei was a havfrue, a maiden of the water meadow, not one of the mørke engler. In a whisper behind her hand, Lisbet had excitedly confided that Lorelei was a princess of the ocean, with glorious long hair, golden like the seaweed that fringed the shores, and large, sad eyes. Lorelei had no family, Lisbet said, and she got terribly lonely. Lisbet was her only friend, which was lucky for Lorelei, thought Freya, because sixteen year old Lisbet had lots of other friends.

"Freya! What are you doing in the water, *lille venn?*" (little friend) called her mother's voice faintly. Freya spun and frowned at the woman leaning over the balcony that ran the width of the white house. Freya raised a finger to her lips, then fiercely waved her mother away. Mamma waved, forced a smile and turned back to the house, no doubt to keep watch from the window. Mamma slept badly and was often awake all night, but Freya couldn't worry about that now. Her eyes greedily searched among the shallows lapping at her legs and beyond, to the tiny rocky islet that emerged when the tide receded. In a couple of hours she could run and stand on it, pretending she lived on a deserted island all by herself, but right now she was hoping there were lots of juicy, delicious fish enticing Lorelei to come and feast. How could it be true that havfrue ate small children? They had all the monkfish, eels, brown trout, grayling and perch to choose from. Freya shook her head, dislodging horrifying images of a beautiful havfrue tearing at the limb of a screaming infant. Havfrue were kind as well as beautiful, Lisbet had said. And Lisbet was hardly ever wrong about anything.

The sky over the peaks above Stranda was the softest mauve-blue now. The wind was still cold, blowing Freya's hair into her eyes. Slowly, she lifted a hand to tuck it behind her ear, afraid any movement would frighten Lorelei away. Shivering, she lifted the wet hem of her flannelette nightie a little higher. Her belly grumbled loudly and she sighed. Why hadn't she thought of grabbing a biscuit or something on her way out the back door? She turned to look at the house, hoping her sister would join her. Why wasn't Lisbet here anyway? Lorelei was *her* special friend after all! She shifted her cramped feet.

"Lazy girl." Freya muttered. A violent shiver gripped her and Freya struggled to keep her breathing even. A tight fear crept into her throat. Surely Lorelei would see her waiting so patiently and come?

"Freya," said a warm, gentle voice right behind her. "Lille venn, why are you standing in that freezing water? You know you'll be having a breathing attack." Freya turned to glare at her mother, who stood perched expertly on the large grey stones of the beach, dressed in a woollen dress and brightly coloured gumboots, a towel draped over her shoulder.

"I'm waiting for…. Something!" Freya replied crossly.

"You are standing in the freezing cold waiting to see a seal? We can see those from the balcony, wrapped warmly in a blanket. *Kom da*, (come on). It's almost breakfast time."

"No, it's… Please, Mamma. Let me…."

"Liebling. Nein." (Darling. No). Mamma always switched to German when she was serious. Dark circles under her eyes meant her patience would be limited today and Freya knew better than to push it. There would be hell to pay from her father if she did. "Kom," said Mamma firmly, reaching out her hands. Mamma's dark blue eyes seemed deep enough to hold safe everything in Freya's world, even the secret desires of her heart. Freya reluctantly stepped out of the water and stumbled into her mother's arms, the warmth of the fluffy, dry towel enfolding her. She glanced one last time at the fjord and thought she saw a stirring of the waters, perhaps the flick of a graceful tail.

CHAPTER TWO

At six thirty next morning Freya and Lisbet sat inside the small roadside hut waiting for the minibus. In the old days the hut was used to house milk churns. Before even their father was born, the churns full of milk would be collected by horse and cart. These days the milk was transported by container truck, which turned off the main road to wind its way down the gravel drive to Askvold, their family dairy. The milk was pumped straight from the big steel milk vats into the refrigerated truck and driven off to catch the early *ferge,* (ferry), to the mainland.

Today the air was cool and fresh with the sweet smell of apple blossom. Spring made everything beautiful and bright. All around them the rich green of new pasture spread like a shaggy rug on which their family's black and white Friesian cows fed, occasionally mooing to each in their deep voices. Little *blåfugl,* (bluebirds) tittered, flashes of bright blue darting between bushes. Yellow-faced flowers sprang up from the dusty verge, nodding their broad, white petal collars. Staring absently, Freya scratched the wooden bench with her finger nails. Until she saw her sister's glare. Normally they would be chattering about everything and anything, giggling and sharing funny impersonations of people they knew and be surprised when the minibus suddenly came to a stop in front of them. But quite suddenly, things had changed. Lisbet seemed upset and cranky about even small things. When Freya complained to Mamma about it, Mamma had smiled wistfully and said, "It's just being a teenager, lille venn. Sometimes it's difficult to be happy. You'll be the same, no doubt." And hugged her tight.

Freya shuffled her shoes on the gravel and stared at the lace curtained windows of the house opposite the road; a blue painted wooden house with white trim, as was the Norwegian custom. Behind the net curtains Old Mrs Horten most likely lingered, but rarely came outside, except when her son Magnus visited from Elveby on the mainland. Freya sighed and shifted her gaze to the lofty expanse of blue sky above the house; so blue and so close she felt as if she could throw a rock and make a hole in it. Maybe this afternoon she would take the rowboat out and look for Lorelei. She didn't want her sister to think she was just a silly little girl, so she said nothing about her disappointment from yesterday. Lately sometimes, Lisbet could snap your head off just for breathing too loud.

The empty minibus pulled up and the girls alighted. Freya frowned as she watched Lisbet march right up front, near Harald the driver, to sit on the single seat, where she knew there was no room for her little sister and sat staring out the window. Freya made her way up to the back seat where they normally sat. She liked being able to see through all the windows, including right down the middle of the bus and through the front windscreen. In about thirty minutes they would have driven almost completely round the island picking up passengers. On a fine day like this the red and blue ferge would be already moored at the tiny wharf, the steel ramp down, ready for cars and trucks to drive straight on. The captain would watch them all from his small wheelhouse up high on the right hand side of the boat as the rumble of the impatient engines vibrated through the steel deck.

Although the ferge was sometimes fun and she would stand at the front, on top deck, feeling the sun and wind on her face, Freya wished they could attend Eikeberg island school, which taught twenty five local students aged seven to fifteen. But this was not acceptable to Freya's father, Torstein, who grew up on Eikeberg and wanted his daughters to have a 'better education.' A larger school would have better resources, he said, not just the chalkboard, books and pencils of Eikeberg Skole. This meant travelling to the mainland. So, each school day morning, Freya and Lisbet left early for their long trip via bus and ferge, to weave around the islands and rocky outcrops of Strandafjord to the large town of Elveby. Then they walked a kilometre up the hill to Elveby school. Every morning as they drove past Eikeberg Skole Freya would stare wistfully at the friendly looking building where all the island children went, except herself and Lisbet. They had been teased about it by island children, especially that tomboy Sigrid and her brother Arvid who said the Askvold family were too posh for the rest of Eikeberg. Freya usually said nothing. What was the point? Pappa's word was law.

Storms in Strandafjord always made them late for school. Sitting in the lounge below decks Freya would fume, while her stomach lurched at every violent pitch and roll of the small ferge as it fought its way through the rough fjord waters. Freya hated the embarrassment of arriving late, hearing the titters of amusement and the whispers of *øyboer,* (islander).

This morning the sky was clear, though the waves chopped and banged at the hull of the little ferge jigging its tight dance at the wharf. As they drove onto the deck, Freya spotted Ragnar the deckhand, in his rough knitted jumper and weatherproof trousers. The winch whined. The ramp rose up then hit the deck with a loud clank, sending shudders through the boat and a tremor of excitement through Freya's breast. A ferge was a big, metal beast with a thumping steel heart you could feel through your feet as you walked on the deck. As she stepped down from the bus she glanced over the tops of the cars. No one new today. She waved at Ragnar, who grinned and waved back as he coiled rope around a steel bollard on the deck. Freya watched her sister Lisbet scowl at something in the distance, her lips tight.

Then, the spell broken, Freya grinned and dashed towards the open door to below decks, gripping the strap of her backpack with one hand, the wooden railing with the other.

"Hey!" shouted Lisbet, running after her. "It's my turn!"

"Not if you can't catch me!" yelled Freya over her shoulder as she clomped down the metal stairs to the low ceilinged room with its brown and orange nylon carpet and rows of mustard yellow plastic seats. Swinging her backpack off her shoulder she sat down on the favoured seat with a good view through the window, just above the waterline. Mr Olsen, an accountant in Elveby, sat in his grey suit reading the paper, one leg over his knee. Old Mrs Vestad, in the same red overcoat, brown stockings and floral dress she'd worn forever, sat with her large shopping bag, checking her list.

Lisbet arrived breathless and fuming to stand over her younger sister.

"Get up. It's my turn!"

"Too bad." Freya dared to stare up at her sister, though her heart was thrashing painfully in her chest. She closed her eyes and willed her breathing to slow. Asthma was such a pain sometimes. Lisbet yanked her by the arm and Freya found herself sprawled on the floor, her bare knees burned on the harsh synthetic carpet, her ears already hot with embarrassment at the stares of the other passengers. Getting to her feet she kicked Lisbet's shin.

"Ow! You stupid little cow!" Lisbet howled, grabbing her leg and rocking, her eyes misted with tears. Freya merely smiled and pushed a strand of hair back from her face. "You wait until I tell Pappa!" Lisbet hissed. But Freya was unrepentant. Planting her feet apart she jammed her hands on her hips and pouted.

"You never came!"

"What are you talking about?" Lisbet screwed up her face.

"Yesterday morning!" Freya said indignantly, jabbing the air with a finger. "You went on and on about how beautiful Lorelei is but you couldn't even be bothered to get out of bed to see her!"

Lisbet lifted her chin at the accusation. "Lorelei knows I sleep in on Tuesdays," she said calmly.

"What?" Freya narrowed her eyes. "You're lying."

"No I'm not. What would you know, Mamma's little baby!"

"Shut up! Just shut your mouth, Lisbet! You don't know anything."

"Well I know something you don't." Lisbet said with an air of superiority. "Lorelei is my friend. She'll never show herself to you."

"Then why did you tell me to get up so early and stand in the freezing cold water?"

Lisbet just smiled and began digging in her bag for a book to read.

"I hate you, Lisbet! You're a horrible, selfish pig!" Freya stomped off to find a seat as far away as possible.

CHAPTER THREE

That afternoon Freya ran home down the dusty driveway from the bus stop without even waiting for Lisbet. She wanted to have as much time as she could before sunset out on the water searching for Lorelei. Once past the field of cows she ploughed on, her head down, frowning in thought as she stomped downhill. Turning right on the narrow path past Gamle Jenny's white house she passed through the corridor of pine trees where the path was strewn with a soft bed of needles and the fresh pinewood smell made you linger. Looking up she saw the open space ahead, a grassy slope where Fjellheim stood proudly overlooking Strandafjord. To the right, behind the house, rose a small hill of beech trees, their round leaves a bright, new green. Among the pale trunks and brown leaf litter on the forest floor Freya had sometimes seen rabbits and sometimes deer. One spring a mother and fawn came to the edge of the forest, not far from the back door. Freya stood, riveted, as they pretended to nibble the short, sweet grass before bounding lightly away back into cover.

In winter time the slope was perfect for sledding. One year Lisbet even skied all the way down to the rocks at the shoreline, shrieking all the way, until she finally leaned sideways a little and slid round to an inelegant stop. Sigrid and Arvid sometimes came over to play. They weren't Freya's favourite friends, but they lived the closest. Sigrid seemed to enjoy teasing Freya about everything, which wore pretty thin after a couple of hours. Then when Freya had enough and went indoors she would have insults and jeers thrown at her back and run straight up to her attic room to cry quietly on her bed.

Life in a small community could be hard sometimes. Everyone knew everything about everyone. Secrets were almost impossible. Which is why the idea of a havfrue as a friend was so deliciously exciting. And Freya had no plans to tell Sigrid about it.

"Freya, where are you going?" asked Mamma curiously as Freya later rushed out the door, backpack on her shoulder.

"Oh, just out in Bestefar's boat for a while. Not long," Freya called as she disappeared round the side of the house. If she kept running Mamma wouldn't have time to follow her with more questions. And, strictly speaking, Freya wasn't breaking any rules because she wasn't *in* the water by herself, unsupervised, she was *on* the water, in her grandfather's little wooden boat.

Down at the shoreline smooth, grey rocks striped with white in all sizes lay tumbled like a giant's toys. Bestefar's green and white rowboat lay on its side, looking forlorn and forgotten. Freya slung her bag onto the middle bench seat then stepped in to open the small compartment at the bow and remove the oarlocks. She dropped them neatly into their iron-ringed holes. Next the oars were positioned held by the oarlocks with their handles facing outwards, paddles resting on the floor of the boat. Hopping out again, Freya pushed and puffed until the row boat broke free of the grass to glide over the rocks and knobbly yellow seaweed into the water.

Her toes loved the crispness of the cold water. The tide was on the turn, so it would be easy to get the row boat out past the little rocky islet. Freya was so intent upon scanning the water for signs of Lorelei that she slipped on the rocks and banged her shin on the edge of the boat. Crying out, she gripped the edge, her knuckles white and waited for the pain to subside to a dull ache as the water swirled around her legs. Nothing was going to stop her from seeing Lorelei. Freya gave one final push and the boat slid out over the water. Scampering inside she lifted an oar from the lock to plunge it to the rocky bottom and push herself further out before settling down to row.

She was quite proud of the fact that she had taught herself to row, after watching Pappa and his brother Onkel Felix rowing out to fish around a larger rocky islet further from shore, home to a permanent colony of seabirds. The brothers always seemed to have such fun when they were alone, just the two of them. It was as if for a short time they were boys again. But as soon as they returned it was back to their usual sombre mood.

Onkel Felix often made fun of Mamma's German accent, though she spoke Norsk fluently. And he never complemented Mamma on her excellent cooking, which everyone else admired. At island community events such as *Syttende Mai,* (17th of May), Mamma's food was always the first to disappear. Sometimes the things Onkel Felix said at the dinner table would have the whole family suddenly go quiet, their heads down, forking food into their mouths. But Mamma never replied. And Pappa didn't speak up in her defence either.

Despite her husband's grumpiness, Tante Nina got along very well with Mamma. The two women would often share recipes at the kitchen table while their husbands washed the dishes. Perhaps it was because Onkel Felix' leg hurt from an accident many years ago. You could see the pain in his face sometimes when he limped inside from the early milking, skin grey as twilight shadows, his hand rubbing the same spot on his leg over and over but giving him no relief. But why was he mean to Mamma? She was the kindest person on Earth.

Freya's efforts had taken her out past Lilleskjæret now. The waters were so clear you could see large rocks on the bottom and small fish darting around. Freya stopped rowing and put up a hand to shield her eyes from the sun. Where would Lorelei appear? She scanned the surface of the calm water. What was that splash there? Oh, just a fish. Or there? She caught sight of something to her right. Oh. Just a bird, swooping low over the surface. It squawked down at her as it flew overhead.

Freya scowled at its retreating form as it disappeared into the distance. She sighed. How had Lisbet even *seen* Lorelei in this vast expanse of deep emerald green?

And then she saw it – a rounded brownish-green shape – emerge slowly to the surface about fifty metres away. It remained unmoving, as if a tiny new island had emerged. It was definitely not a seal, Freya decided firmly. She stared, keeping perfectly still so as not to frighten it. Was that a pair of eyes, blinking at her? Freya couldn't see clearly from this distance. Yes! It was definitely a pair of eyes, which turned up at the outer edges. Blinked slowly. Then the head began to slide back down into the deep. Freya leapt to her feet.

"Wait!" she called out, as the havfrue disappeared. "Come back! Please!" Freya's foot became tangled in the rope lying in the bottom of the boat. "Lorelei! I just want to ask you... Argh!" Freya tried lifting her foot to shake it free of the rope, all the while struggling to maintain her balance and her gaze on the exact spot she'd seen the havfrue. But she overbalanced, flung out her hand to steady herself and missed the sturdy wooden rim, toppling overboard into the frigid waters. Her muscles immediately seized up from the cold and she began to sink. Freya gasped, sucking in salty water and forced her arms and legs to move. Struggling wildly she reached out to the boat bobbing beside her. Salty water splashed into her mouth. She swallowed, panting and crying. Her chest felt tight. Her breaths were tiny and painful. She fought the panic of an asthma attack. She was a pretty good swimmer but the cold made her arms ache and numb. Her legs thrashed below, trying to get a rhythm going. She reached again for the boat but the freeboard, the side, was too high, designed to carry heavy loads. She screamed, swivelling to see if Mamma was outside, at the washing line perhaps, but the house sat stolidly staring back at her, basking in the afternoon sun. Lisbet would be indoors, listening to her radio. Freya panted, each breath becoming heavier. Making her way awkwardly to the stern she gripped the transom, knowing she was too weak to haul herself into the safety of the boat. The tide was moving swiftly now, taking her towards the shore. If she could just hold on, the water itself would save her.

When her feet first struck rocks Freya cried in relief. Still weeping, she pushed the boat to the shore, struggling over the slippery rocks and seaweed, weighed down by her soaked clothes. Shivering violently she dragged her feet up the slope, which now seemed like a mountain.

"Freya!" cried Mamma's frantic voice. The welcome thud of her footsteps running downhill towards Freya brought a wave of relief. Exhausted, Freya slumped to the ground, unable to speak.

CHAPTER FOUR

Freya felt a warm hand on her forehead. With supreme effort she opened her very heavy eyes. The urge to sleep was so strong, like a riptide. She wanted to fall back into the blissfulness and forget the awful accident, the searing cold.

"Oh, lille venn, what happened?" Mamma asked softly, her eyes huge with worry.

"I..." Freya tried to tell her but a coughing fit took over. Mamma reached for the puffer on the bedside table.

"Here."

Freya shook the plastic container ten times, pressed the button and breathed in, trying to keep her tongue out of the way. Asthma meds tasted bitter. But they certainly made a difference when you needed them.

She leaned back on the pillows and handed Mamma the puffer. Her face suddenly felt hot with shame.

"I'm so sorry Mamma!"

"But what were you doing out there on the water? All by yourself? You know how dangerous the fjord can be. The weather is so changeable."

"I just... I just wanted to..." Freya stared out of her little attic window at the small fluffy clouds scuttling by and imagined Lorelei floating on her back smiling up at the sun. Turning back to her mother's kind face she wished she could confide her secret. But adults often just smiled wistfully and dismissed such things as the colourful imagination of childhood. How could her mother understand how deeply and passionately Freya wished to befriend the beautiful maiden of the water meadow? No one in the history of Eikeberg Island had ever befriended a havfrue, a lovely mystery of the deep. To be the first and only one to have a havfrue as a friend, a soul mate, a confidante – how special! Then it wouldn't matter what Lisbet said or did. Freya could tell her dearest friend, Lorelei, and feel understood. It wouldn't matter what Sigrid said or did, how much she teased, how cruel her comments, knowing Freya could simply run down to the water and call on her friend would wipe away all the hurt and pain and loneliness.

"Freya? Lille venn, what is it? What is it you are trying so hard not to tell me?" Mamma stroked Freya's face, gently brushing hair away from her eyes. It was the touch of babyhood, of that special time between mother and child that could never be named, one which both knew would last forever. Freya stared at her mother's face, at the deep blue eyes, the chestnut brown hair she wore in a long, thick plait that hung beside her neck, at the graceful arc of her brows and the long dark lashes, at the strong Germanic jawline. Mamma's face spoke of her character – kindness and strength you could rely on.

"Lisbet said if I went down to the water at five in the morning I would see a havfrue, a Lorelei." Freya hung her head. "Please don't be mad at me, Mamma! I only wanted a special friend."

Mamma smiled. Her eyes crinkled at the edges. She squeezed Freya's hand.

"I understand, child. This is about Sigrid, isn't it? She upsets you."

"Yes. But it's not just her, Mamma. All the children at school call us øyboer, as if we are dirty, scruffy little dogs that no one likes."

Mamma frowned. "They say this to you? This is how they treat you at that school?"

"Mamma, please, I don't want any trouble. If you say something to the teacher it will just get worse."

"But I must protect you, lille venn. It's my job as your mother." She shook her head, her blue eyes hardened. "I know what it is like to be an outsider," she said softly, gazing out the window. Freya watched her mother closely, knowing she was speaking about being German and living in Norway. In World War II the Germans had invaded Norway, forcing people to work for them, rounding up those who refused and sending them to prison where many were abused and often starved. Freya's grandfather, Petter Askvold, had been forced to drive his lorry for the enemy seven days a week and ended up in prison where he witnessed terrible cruelty by the German guards. It was a whole generation since the war had ended but bad feelings persisted, bad feelings and distrust of German people.

"I need to trust you, Freya," Mamma said firmly. "I need to know, deep down in my bones, that you will not take Bestefar's boat out by yourself again. It's too dangerous." Mamma tapped Freya's hand. "Freya? Are you listening to me? I can see by your face that you are thinking why you should not be allowed to do this. You are thinking your Mamma is too strict. You are feeling resentful. Isn't this true?"

"But Mamma, I only wanted to see Lorelei. I just needed to. My heart is breaking and I know Lorelei will understand! Please don't stop me from looking for her!" Freya cried, tears in her eyes.

"Freya," Mamma said firmly. "You are not to go out in the boat again, do you understand? It is too dangerous. You are too young."

Freya felt the anger rise inside her, flooding over her cheeks in a hot wave.

"Mamma, I can look after myself! I'm not a little child anymore!" A deep cough gripped her chest and she leaned over to get air. Mamma's warm hand made circles on her back until the coughing ceased.

"Freya, Lorelei are not real, much as you would love a special friend. I'm sorry. It's just a dream."

"I knew you wouldn't believe me!" Freya said angrily.

"Freya, this isn't about Lorelei. This is about you, my child, being in danger. Don't you remember the legends? Of the children drowning? Can you not understand that I want to keep my own child safe?" Mamma's voice was wobbly, her German accent quavered into higher notes, like the song of a frightened bird at night. "Please, Freya. Do as I ask."

Freya's mind searched for other ways she could look for Lorelei. Other ways she could explore the water without strictly disobeying Mamma's rule. There had to be a way. Lorelei was real!

"I promise, Mamma, I will not take the boat out again," Freya said quietly.

Mamma smiled and kissed Freya's forehead.

"Thank you, Liebling, my good little girl. I love you."

"Love you too, Mamma."

"I should be leaving you now to sleep. You're still very tired. There are dark circles under your eyes. And I'm worried about that cough."

Freya snuggled down into the warm doona.

"I'll be fine, Mamma. Don't worry about me. I won't do anything silly like run around outside in my nightie." She giggled.

Mamma went to the door.

"Good. Sleep well, lille venn. Pappa will be in to see you later."

***

When Freya woke the next morning the sun blazed through her attic window casting shadows over the colourful floor rug. Birds chatted to each other in the beech forest behind the house. Freya breathed deep, feeling relaxed, her breathing even. Of all the rooms upstairs the four small attic rooms under the eaves were the most cosy, where the smell of pine on the walls, floor and ceiling infused you with a sense of calm. Perhaps many other children had slept in this very room. Freya's grandparents, Petter and Hilde Askvold had moved here after the war. Before that Fjellheim had belonged to the Vestad family, whose lineage in this part of Norway stretched back to the days of King Harald Herdebrei and the battle fought on the island in the year 1162. Freya loved reading about the history of her country, even though some of it made her feel sad, that a war could last a hundred and ten years. As she lay snug in her bed, Freya imagined herself a princess, King Harald's daughter. And then she imagined Harald the minibus driver as the king and giggled to herself.

Footsteps came up the stairs at the front of the house, continued over the landing, past the main rooms towards her. Freya's bedroom door opened. Lisbet folded her arms and leaned against the door frame.

"You're pathetic, you know that? Wanting Mamma's attention all the time. Well, you've really done it now. She's terrified of letting you out of her sight. Good one!"

"What do you mean?" Demanded Freya angrily, the happy thoughts vanished, as they so often did these days when Lisbet was around.

"Why are you so selfish? Don't you realise that your stupid actions affect the rest of us?"

"I didn't do anything stupid!" Cried Freya. "Why are you so mean to me Lisbet?"

"I'm just telling you the truth. But you're such a baby you still believe in legends and dreams." Lisbet flicked her golden hair off her shoulder.

"You mean Lorelei?" Freya sat up in bed. "I thought she was your friend?"

Lisbet smirked.

"I just told you that story to see if you would believe me." She laughed. "And you did! You actually got up at five o'clock in the morning and stood in the water in your nightie, like the idiot you are."

"I trusted you!" Freya cried, tears in her eyes. "You're supposed to be my big sister! You're supposed to look after me, not punish me for nothing or behave so mean to me for no reason."

"No reason?" Lisbet retorted angrily. She swung her fist violently into the wall. "What do you know about it?" She shouted, her voice shrill, her eyes glittering with rage. Turning on her heel she stomped away to her own room and slammed the door. Freya sat, mouth open in shock at Lisbet's outburst, then buried her head in the pillow and sobbed for the big sister she used to know, the one used to laugh with her, the one who used to tell her she was a 'funny, amusing little thing'. The big sister who had been her friend and protector.

"Freya?" Her father's voice said from the doorway. "What's wrong?" He sat on the edge of her bed and held her close. Within Pappa's arms Freya felt safe again, but sadness had crept into her heart. Something was terribly wrong with Lisbet. And Freya didn't know where to begin to try and help her.

"Are you feeling better?" Pappa asked, lifting her chin to smile at her. "That was a bit of an adventure, out on the fjord Bestefar's boat, wasn't it?"

Freya nodded. "I'm sorry. I know I did the wrong thing. The water was so cold Pappa! My legs went numb and my arms ached so much!"

Pappa grinned and kissed her cheek.

"That's because you are not meant to be living in such cold water. Only mørke engler live in the fjord, in such dark, cold places. They are not for you, *vennen min.*"

Freya sniffed. "You believe in them? You believe they live in the water?"

"Well…" He smiled and his eyes slid sideways.

"Mamma says they are just a dream! But Lisbet told me Lorelei lives there and I wanted to meet her. So I took Bestefar's boat. I thought I would be safe Pappa!"

"And did you see this famous Lorelei?"

"Yes! I am sure I did. I saw her head come up out of the water. I saw her blink at me! It was amazing!"

"Then you are a very lucky little girl," said Pappa, chuckling. "And now," he said pulling back the bedcovers. "It's time to get up. I will see you downstairs."

Freya dressed in a daze. Somehow she must get down to the water again. Today. Perhaps she could call the havfrue to the shore. But how did you do that?

CHAPTER FIVE

Freya jumped down from the minibus and ran towards home, her rucksack bouncing on her back, her eyes fixed firmly on the fjord ahead of her. The afternoon sun shone brilliantly on the water, sparkling and glorious. On the other side of the fjord dark mountains rose majestically. The rounded mountain named Bollen, so named because it looked like a bread roll, sat like a friendly faced troll having a bath. Behind Bollen the fjord continued inland. Directly opposite Fjellheim the small township of Stranda glinted in the afternoon light. The sharp slopes behind the town rose quickly into jagged, tooth like precipices where snow adorned the peaks even in summer.

White pear tree blossom blew gently across her path like summer snow as Freya ran down towards

Gamle Jenny's white wooden house. Lisbet had in the past visited Gamle Jenny every week for piano lessons, but even that didn't seem to please her these days. Freya's pace slowed as she walked through the narrow alley of pine trees, breathing in the fresh scent and kicking pinecones with glee. There, ahead, stood her home, where it had been for well over a hundred years, nestled into the slope facing the fjord, with the small, neat woods sheltering it from behind. Was there ever a more beautiful place on earth? wondered Freya. She glanced at the water down by the rounded grey rocks at the shoreline. No ripples. Disappointed, she ran the rest of the way home, her bag jostling on her back as if it too couldn't wait to get indoors.

After a drink and a cookie Freya changed into her outdoor clothes and respectfully asked her mother if she could go down to the fjord, but not into the water. Her mother stroked her hair and smiled.

"Of course. Just don't stay too long. The air is still chilly even though spring has arrived in all her glory."

Joyfully, Freya skipped down the grassy slope and perched herself on a large rock. Greedily, her eyes searched the water. Today it was smooth as glass and she imagined her father and Uncle Felix would love to have water skied behind the small power boat which was kept in the little red boat house. In summertime it was as if the water called to the children all day long while they sat in the classroom dreaming of swimming and making rafts from bits of wood they found washed up on the shore. Last year Lisbet had excelled herself with her intricate lashings of rope which had successfully transformed odd planks of wood into a make-believe boat. Unfortunately they had forgotten to bring it up onto the beach and a few days later a sudden storm had taken it away.

Freya was tempted to take off her shoes and socks and paddle in the water but the memory of the cold and numbness in her limbs was enough to dissuade her. Out there, somewhere, Lorelei swam, gliding through the water, her golden hair streaming behind her. Freya's heart beat faster with excitement. Today! Today she would meet her new friend.

But how did you call to a havfrue?

Freya tilted back her head and began to sing a lullaby her mother had sung to her every night when Freya was small. It was about a blue bird that flew into a house through the window. It was a song of spring and of joy. Freya hoped her voice was sweet enough to draw Lorelei's attention. By the time she had sung the chorus twice and embarked on the first verse again Freya began to have doubts and her voice wavered. Perhaps it was the wrong song? She switched to another song, *'Alle Fugler'* which they had learned in school. This was also about birds, all the little birds of spring which come back to the land with the warmer weather. At school they had been divided into two groups, with one group singing the harmony. At the school concert the audience had clapped enthusiastically as the children finished the performance. Now Freya sang the first verse and was onto the second when she heard a splash.

There! A ripple, out in the middle of the fjord. Freya stopped singing and watched as the ripple drew closer. Was that a fin? And then the ripples ceased. A

rounded shape, a havfrue's head, rose. Freya shot to her feet.

"Lorelei! I'm Freya," she called. "I've been waiting for you!"

The head was so far away and so dark that Freya could not see Lorelei's eyes but she knew in her heart what she was looking at. A princess of the deep! A mythical being no one had ever seen in person! Freya felt she was the luckiest girl in the history of Norway.

And then Lorelei slid back beneath the water. Rings spread out for a moment, then disappeared into nothing.

"No... Please come back!" Freya searched the smooth surface frantically. "There's so much I want to know. There's so much I want to tell you, Lorelei!" But the only answer was the soft shooshing of the water lapping at her shoes as the tide came in. Freya sat a while, until the wind turned sour and she felt a shiver. Dispirited, she stood and turned to leave, casting one final, longing glance at the water, but there was no sign a havfrue had ever graced its surface. A seagull squawked above and landed nearby, regarding her with its bright yellow eye as if to say, "I told you so."

They had Laks fish for dinner with creamy mashed potato, peas and white sauce. It was Freya's favourite but she could barely concentrate on eating. Her disappointment jangled around inside her head.

For the rest of that week Freya rushed home every afternoon to sit by the shoreline and sing to Lorelei, but no matter how long she sat or how sweetly she sang there was no sign of the havfrue again.

Freya's twelfth birthday was a week away. There were many things she hoped to get, such as a new bicycle and lots of books about mermaids and old Norwegian myths and legends. She thought that perhaps if she had more knowledge she would know what to do.

It was Saturday, the morning of the sixth of May, Freya's birthday. Sleepily she opened her eyes and stared at the sloping pine ceiling of her attic bedroom. She had recently stuck some old calendar pictures with sticky tape overhead - pictures of the fjord, pictures of people in national dress costume smiling happily on a hillside of daisies, pictures of people bathing or diving from pontoons into the sparkling fjord. With hope in her heart Freya got dressed and went downstairs. The house was very quiet. There were no breakfast smells. Everyone was still in bed. Freya glanced at the clock and realised it was only six am. Pappa and Onkel Felix would be in the middle of the morning milking. But where were her birthday presents? Where were the decorations? Freya lifted the cake tin lid and peered inside. It was empty. A churning feeling began in her stomach and her face flushed hot. No one had remembered she was turning twelve years old today! With a sob Freya opened the back door and ran outside, stumbling down to the shore.

Across the fjord a pale pink sky heralded another glorious spring day. A light breeze lifted her long hair around her face and cooled her cheeks. Sitting on the rock she pulled her nightie down over her knees and wept. The echo of her sobs came back to her across the water, as if a sad twin cried too. Sniffing, she wiped her nose on her sleeve. Out of habit she scanned the water for signs of Lorelei.

And then she heard it - a splash over to her left. Gulping, she sat very still, slowly turning her head. Another splash and a big tail fin broke the surface, closer than before. Suddenly, a naked lady drew up out of the water smoothly and slowly like a majestic queen. She pulled herself up to sit on a large rock not far away. Freya stared wordlessly. The havfrue stared back, flicking her slick, yellow hair from her shoulders. Her skin was very pale with a greenish tinge, right down past her waist, but the bottom half of her was dark green and purplish scales. Her slender body tapered to a long, long tail ending in a large frilly fin. Freya's gaze travelled up to the havfrue's strange face. Lorelei's eyes were large and set far apart. She had two sets of eyelids - one set swept down and up again, the second set was underneath those and swept from the outside into the middle and back again. The colour of Lorelei's eyes was hard to detect. They seemed a murky greenish colour, perhaps a light brown and the pupils were similar to a goat's – the irises vertical and elongated.

Freya's skin felt prickly all over. Thoughts and words tumbled around inside her head like autumn leaves caught in a whirly-whirly. Lorelei was here! Freya was desperate not to ruin this moment.

The havfrue sat silently staring back at Freya. She had a sharp, pointed chin, high cheekbones and a broad forehead. The sun glistened off her hair which seemed like something between strands of thin seaweed and coarse hair, like a horse's tail. Freya took a deep breath and decided it was now or never.

"My name is Freya and I am so happy to meet you," she said quietly, watching Lorelei's face intently.

"I have so many questions!" Her voice grew excited and despite her best intentions not to frighten Lorelei, the words scrambled out like wild rabbits. "Where did you come from? Where do you live? Are there more like you? Do you have a mum and dad? How old are you? What do you eat for…"

Lorelei opened her small mouth and a sharp sound came out, like a chicken squawk. Freya was so shocked she stopped talking, which, as her Mum would say, was a miracle. Lorelei squawked again.

"I'm sorry," Freya said, with her palms turned upwards. "I don't understand you. I wish I did." Freya took in every detail of Lorelei's appearance, drinking it into her memory so that she would never forget. Lorelei's completely flat chest had no nipples at all. Her chest was taut, the ribs and ligaments showing. Soft folds of skin under her long, thin arms joined to her torso like large webbing. Or wings. Freya had a vision of Lorelei gliding through the water at top speed, chasing fish.

"Well I can see you're definitely not a Disney mermaid," Freya remarked with a smile. Lorelei's head tilted to one side as she listened. "For one thing, you don't need a clamshell bikini top to cover… anything. Does this mean you don't have babies? You don't breastfeed?"

Lorelei squawked again and pointed to the water with her long finger, her strange eyes glittering like bits of amber glass. She doubled blinked slowly, waiting.

Freya nodded. "I see. You have to go?"

In a flash, Lorelei slid back into the water and was gone.

"Lorelei," Freya whispered, her shining eyes

staring at the gentle ripples emanating from the spot the havfrue had disappeared. She hardly dared believe it wasn't all a dream. "My friend," she said, clasping her hands together, feeling the joy bubble up inside her. "The best birthday present ever!"

CHAPTER SIX

Later that morning Freya's birthday celebrations started to take shape. She helped Mamma decorate the kitchen with colourful paper streamers and balloons. The *bløtkake*, the lightest, fluffiest sponge cake in the world, had been baked fresh that day. Mamma was an expert at producing the two identical soft, round sponges, which she stuck together with thick layers of whipped cream and home-made strawberry jam. Then the entire cake was covered in whipped cream and topped with fresh apricot halves, grapes, strawberries and blueberries. It was the largest cake Freya had ever seen and her tummy gurgled with anticipation. She reminded herself that she would need to leave plenty of room for a nice big slice. Tante Nina, unusually pale today, was helping with the dishes. Mamma insisted she go into the lounge room and put her feet up. The two women exchanged a look that Freya could not interpret but she was too excited to ask what it meant. It was her birthday! The best day of the year. And she had made friends with a real live havfrue. Nothing on earth could spoil this day. Even if she got the worst presents ever. As she laid the table Freya sang *Alle Fugler,* the song which had brought Lorelei to her.

"My, you are a happy little bird today, Freya!" Said Mamma, smiling, as she placed a large wooden trivet on the table.

"I've had the best day already, Mamma!" Freya said. "Lorelei came to see me. Finally! She must have known it was my birthday! How amazing is that? I'm the only girl in the whole of Norway who has actually met a havfrue." She giggled excitedly.

Mamma smiled and brushed Freya's cheek with her hand.

"I'm so glad you're happy, lille venn. Birthdays are for happiness."

At five thirty the back door opened and Onkel Felix and Pappa came in from the afternoon milking, smelling of silage and cow dung, despite removing their muddy boots and coveralls in the *ingangen,* (airlock porch). Pappa kissed Mamma's cheek and rubbed his hands together as he stood near the stove warming them. Onkel Felix stood awkwardly by the back door, his eyes scanning the room.

"I suppose Nina isn't here?"

"She's lying down in the lounge room," Mamma said, indicating with a wooden spoon.

Wordlessly, Onkel Felix walked past them and into the adjoining room. Freya felt a cold cloud had entered the kitchen, smothering her joy a little. Mamma seemed tense. Pappa stroked her cheek and announced he was going to have a shower. Freya heard his feet climb the creaky staircase to the second floor to the bathroom under the eaves where the shower had been installed only five years earlier. It was a simple life at Fjellheim. Until recently they'd only been able to have baths, something else for Sigrid to tease her about, Freya thought sullenly.

"What's wrong, lille venn?" Mamma said.

Freya shook her head. "Nothing." She went to the drawer where the pretty serviettes were kept and counted out six white ones with pink and purple wildflowers. Arranging them on each plate she stood back and admired her handiwork. The table looked fabulous, especially the small vase of wildflowers in the centre of the white tablecloth. Even Onkel Felix wasn't going to spoil things.

"Would you call Lisbet please, Freya?"

Freya skipped to the staircase, leapt up the stairs two at a time and knocked on her sister's door.

"Lisbet? It's dinnertime! Birthday dinner time!"

"Go away," came the voice from within.

"But Mamma said…"

"All right! Stop nagging me. Go away!"

"Can't you at least be nice to me on my birthday?" Freya said quietly to herself as she turned away.

Later, as they sat down to eat, Pappa exclaimed over the food. Freya had chosen sausages, mash, gravy, broccoli and *tyttebær* (cranberry) jelly. Even Tante Nina managed to eat a small portion. Onkel Felix grunted his approval, only when his wife insisted, digging him with her elbow. Lisbet ate in silence. Her parents glanced worriedly at each other but no one dared to question her. It was like a spell. If you said something, you broke the spell and then everyone would feel angry and sad. So if you said nothing and just ignored her, you could pretend everything was okay. Pappa talked about the cows, the two new calves born and told Freya with a wink that he was going to name one of them after her as a special birthday privilege.

"Thank you Pappa," Freya said, grinning. "I bet she's beautiful and very well behaved."

Pappa chuckled. "Of course!"

"She's a sweet little thing," Mamma remarked.

"Just like me!" Freya said with a giggle. Even Tante Nina smiled at that. Lisbet snorted in her throat and delicately placed a morsel of food into her mouth. Onkel Felix scowled down at his plate, sawing away at a sausage.

"Can't keep it anyway," he said tersely. "Don't know why you bothered naming it, brother."

Tante Nina gave Freya a sad smile of apology.

Freya tried to lighten things. "The best is yet to come, you know! The most beautiful, enormous bløtkake is coming. You love bløtkake, don't you Onkel Felix?"

"Too sweet," he replied, getting up and pushing his chair in, leaving his dirty plate on the table. His wife watched him as he flung open the back door and strode out into the dark.

Turning to Freya she said, "Sorry Freya. Your uncle is feeling sore today."

"His leg again?" Freya asked.

"Yes." Tante Nina hung her head.

"Is there nothing a doctor could do?"

"No." Tante Nina looked at Mamma. There was a hint of something in her eyes, something Freya didn't understand.

"Now, now, Freya," said Mamma briskly. "It's your birthday! A happy day." She got up and opened the fridge. The glorious cream covered cake looked even bigger somehow! Proudly she placed it in the centre of the table and handed the cutting knife to Freya. "Now stand up, lille venn and make a wish."

Freya looked at her mother, eyes wide. "I can use the big knife?" She said.

Mamma nodded. "You're ready. You're twelve now."

Freya carefully sank the tip of the large knife right in the centre, deep, deep into the luscious cake, then pulled it towards herself. Plunging the knife in again she cut a large slice.

Pappa chuckled. "Now that's what I call a slice of cake!"

"Pig," Lisbet said under her breath.

"Lisbet…" Pappa warned.

"Well she is! Don't you get it?" Lisbet snapped.

Freya stared at her sister. She had never seen her so insolent towards Pappa. The knife fell to the plate the clatter.

"What's wrong with you Lisbet? Why are you so horrible? Especially on my birthday! Can't you even be nice for one minute?"

"Freya!" Mamma cried.

"Come on girls," Pappa intervened.

"Well I'm sick of her! She doesn't care about anyone except herself!" Freya yelled and ran to the stairs.

Scrambling up the wooden steps she slipped and skinned her shin, cried out in pain and disappointment, then rushed to her room and slammed the door. Her birthday was ruined.

CHAPTER SEVEN

On Sunday morning Freya woke early, the sun streaming in through her attic window, creating a prism of colours through the glass reflected on the ceiling. Freya dressed quickly and crept downstairs. Grabbing herself a couple of cookies and a small bottle she filled with milk she set out to find Lorelei.

The sun had no warmth in it. As Freya perched herself comfortably on one of the rounded rocks she felt the cold seep through her clothes but, undeterred, she nibbled on a biscuit and drank some milk before settling herself to sing.

Within moments Lorelei appeared close by, the top of her head and her eyes visible above the surface of the water as she glided smoothly towards Freya. Absolute joy buzzed in Freya's heart. As before, Lorelei drew herself up to sit on a rock nearby and watched Freya silently, her eyes double blinking slowly.

"It was my birthday yesterday, you know," chatted Freya. Then her mood darkened. "And my stupid sister ruined it. Even Onkel Felix was grumpy, but that's not unusual for him."

Lorelei tilted her head on the side, listening intently.

"I don't understand my family sometimes," Freya said sadly, shaking her head. "Onkel Felix has a beautiful wife, Tante Nina. Lisbet has lots of friends. Why can't they just be happy? Even Mamma seemed a bit sad last night and Pappa tried to smooth things over. But you know," Freya sat up, feeling indignant. "It's just not fair! It was *my* birthday and they didn't even *try* to be happy!"

Lorelei scratched at her long slender arm, picking something from the scales. Then whatever it was she had found she put in her mouth and nibbled at it with her sharply pointed, gleaming white teeth. Freya watched, mesmerised. Then Lorelei rubbed her almost flat nose with her hand and began finger combing her hair. She stared across the fjord intently, her eyes narrowed as if she saw something. Freya's gaze tried to follow but she saw nothing except the smooth water. In the distance to their right a white tourist ship travelled slowly in front of the small township of Stranda and headed up the fjord past Bollen.

"Do those tourist ships worry you, Lorelei?" asked Freya. "Do they have big propellers that could hurt you?"

Lorelei turned to look at Freya and opened her mouth. A harsh, deep guttural sound came out.

"Hm. I guess you're not that impressed with them then."

Lorelei leaned over and spat into the water a glob of green mucus. Freya screwed up her face in disgust at first, but then thought that havfrue manners were probably different to human manners.

"I've been thinking about telling Gamle Jenny about you, seeing as Mamma and Pappa and definitely Lisbet don't believe in you. My parents just smile and say things like, "That's nice." It's ridiculous! You are *real!* But perhaps you only want to appear to me? I'm your special friend, right? I don't want to share you with anyone." Freya picked up the bottle of milk and another cookie and offered it to Lorelei. "Would you like to try some human food?" Freya inched off her rock very slowly looking down to place her feet carefully as she moved towards the havfrue. "It's delicious, you know. The milk is totally fresh, straight from the cow, pretty much. It's from yesterday's milking. And the cookies were baked by my Mamma. I'm sure you'll like them. Although... They don't have any fish in them."

Lorelei's large dark eyes watched Freya approaching, watched every movement and stared curiously at the bottle of milk and the cookie held out towards her. At last Freya was close enough that Lorelei could reach out and take the milk and cookie, but disappointingly, she started grooming her tail, picking out bits and pieces and crunching on them. Being this close to the havfrue Freya could smell the sea on her, the salty tang of seaweed, the fishy smell, which wasn't completely unpleasant, however strange. Lorelei's long hair spread over her shoulders and back like strips of thin cloth. The tiniest pointed white shells and blue rounded limpets stuck to the strands like colourful beads.

"Maybe you think it's not food?" Freya said taking a nibble from the cookie and a small sip from the bottle. "See? It's yummy. You try it." She held out the items to Lorelei again. This time Lorelei took them from Freya's hands. Her long fingers had no fingernails. She stared at the bottle from all angles, then tipped it up, sending the white liquid splashing onto the rocks. She put the bottle up to her eye and stared around her wonderingly. She looked inside the bottle, right through the base, at Freya on the other end and doubled blinked, making clicking noises with her tongue. Then she used the cookie to rub on her body.

"No!" Freya laughed out loud. "That's not what it's for. You *eat* it." She mimed the action of putting it in her mouth. Lorelei looked down at the sludgy mess and picked off a tiny chocolate chip which she then put in her mouth and chewed with her pointy teeth. Grimacing, she spat it out. Staring at Freya, she squawked once, then disappeared, leaving only the song of the seagulls and the gentle splash and gurgle of water.

Freya sighed happily. Lorelei was so funny! It was like making friends with someone from another country. Or another planet. How curious and interesting the havfrue was! Like no one Freya had ever met before. She felt very, very special. Gathering the empty bottle and cramming the last of the cookies into her mouth, Freya got to her feet and walked up the slope to Gamle Jenny's house.

Freya's grandparents on her father's side were long dead and her German grandparents, Oma and Opa, didn't like to travel, so Gamle Jenny was the closest Freya had to a grandparent.

As with all the homes on Eikeberg island, the front of the house faced the fjord. Most homes were at least a hundred years old, made of wood and painted many times over the years. The really old houses and huts were made of thick slabs of timber and had been coated with a special oil over the centuries which stained them a dark brown. Some of the huts up in the blueberry forest were almost 800 years old. Gamle Jenny's house was painted white with three upstairs windows and three downstairs windows facing the fjord. On the side facing Fjellheim, Freya's home, was an attic window and below that the kitchen window. Gamle Jenny's light was always on in the kitchen. She liked to bake and would often pop around to her neighbours with treats she wanted to share. It had been a couple of weeks since Freya had seen Gamle Jenny and she wondered if the old lady was okay. Normally she would have brought a special birthday treat for the birthday person at Fjellheim. Freya walked around to the back door which was sheltered from the weather by a tiny porch. She wiped her feet carefully then knocked on the door. It always took a while for Gamle Jenny to get to the door so Freya waited patiently. The old lady opened the door slowly. The first thing Freya saw was her slippered feet, then the colourful floral apron and finally the beautiful, friendly face. Gamle Jenny's pure white hair was swept up into her usual neat bun.

"I thought I saw you running up the slope," said Gamle Jenny in her soft voice. "Good morning Miss

Freya. And happy birthday for yesterday. I'm so sorry I couldn't visit you yesterday but my daughter came and, as you know, she doesn't visit as frequently as she used to. Anna is now a very busy woman, working for a newspaper in Oslo. Come in! Come in and sit. I have a small surprise for you."

Freya carefully removed her boots leaving them at the door and followed the old lady to the front room where comfortable rose pink sofas gathered around the wood heater. Large windows faced the fjord. An entire wall was almost covered with framed photos of her family. School photos of her grandchildren from every year were proudly displayed along with wedding photos of her children Anna, Jakob and Lene. Freya loved this room, with its plush carpet, soft woollen knee blankets and hand stitched cushions. It spoke of love and care over the years and tradition which was very important to the people on Eikeberg island. There were several traditional hand carved wooden items around the room painted the special Norway blue and adorned with *rosemaling*, painted roses, such as a plate, a small bowl and a matchbox dispenser which hung on the wall above the wood heater. Freya settled into one of the armchairs and waited. Soon Gamle Jenny appeared from the kitchen carrying a chocolate cake topped with multi-coloured candles. She placed it on a side table next to Freya and struck a match.

"Now, Freya, make a wish. And make it a good one." The dancing flames reflected in Gamle Jenny's pale blue eyes as her knobbly old fingers lit each candle carefully. Freya took a deep breath closed her eyes and blew, wishing with all her heart that Gamle Jenny would believe her about Lorelei. "And now, a small gift." Gamle Jenny pulled a small wrapped package from her apron pocket.

"Thank you so much!" Freya said. Her nimble fingers undid the ribbon and paper. There, lying in her palm, was a small wooden box with a symbol she had never seen before carved in the lid. It was a curved, flowing symbol, like a fish hook combined with a mermaid's tail. Freya opened the box and inside was a silver charm of a mermaid on a silver chain. "Oh my goodness! It's beautiful!"

"The box was given to me on my twelfth birthday," Gamle Jenny said.

"I love it!" Freya exclaimed, tracing the carved symbol with her finger tip.

"Would you like me to put it on you?" Gamle Jenny said.

"Yes please!" Freya turned her back to the old lady and felt her hair being gently lifted from her shoulders. She saw the dazzling silver mermaid on the chain briefly in front of her eyes before it was gently laid against her skin. She spun round to hug the old lady tightly. "You are so *snill,* (kind) to me," she said.

Gamle Jenny's eyes misted over. "You're like a grandchild to me, Freya. You and Lisbet both, although I haven't seen Lisbet for piano lessons for quite a few weeks now."

"Yes, I don't know what's wrong with her,"

Gamle Jenny looked concerned. "Is she unwell? Has something happened?"

Freya stared out the window. "I don't know. But something is going on and no one wants to talk about it."

She turned to look at the old lady's kind face. "But the worst thing is she's so mean to me," she said quietly. Gamle Jenny sat beside her and took Freya's hands into her lap. She squeezed them gently.

"Sisters can be hard to understand at times. I had three of them," she said, her eyes twinkling.

"What I don't understand, is that if she is upset why doesn't she just tell us what's wrong?"

"Sometimes that's the hardest thing to do," Gamle Jenny said. "Now, would you like a drink? Some Solo perhaps?"

"Yes, thank you. You know how much I love *brus*!" Freya giggled. "It goes right up my nose!" As the old lady handed her a small bottle of yellow fizzy drink Freya twisted the top and gulped down the sweet liquid. "See?" And she giggled again, wiping her nose as delicately as she could. Gamle Jenny settled herself with a cup of tea.

"So, what's new in your life little Freya?" Gamle Jenny trained her twinkly blue eyes on Freya, almost as if she knew the delicious secret.

"Well, I have a new friend," said Freya, feeling the joy bubble up inside her again. Her fingers touched the silver mermaid pendant. "And it's a secret."

"A secret? Does this mean you cannot tell me? I do so love secrets!" The old lady sipped her tea, grinning.

"Well, I was just saying to Lorelei this morning that I should tell you about her," said Freya. Then clapped a hand over her mouth. She'd gone and said it!

"Lorelei?" The old lady said, her head tilted to the side. "You mean a havfrue?" The smile had vanished from her face. Freya felt a cold tingly feeling in her tummy.

"Um, yes. A havfrue. I call her Lorelei, because that's what they're called in Germany, Mamma says."

"I see," Gamle Jenny, said taking another sip. "And is Lorelei friendly? Has she tried to hurt you in anyway?"

"Oh no! Lorelei would never do that!" Freya exclaimed. "She is my best friend in the whole world. No one else I know has ever had a havfrue for a best friend." She sipped her Solo, feeling flutters of happiness inside her chest. "I thought of telling you because I thought you would understand, and you would believe, just like I do, because no one else at home does. It's like they don't even *want* to believe."

"You do need to be very careful, Freya," warned Gamle Jenny, her pale eyes serious.

"Why?"

"Because havfrue are not people like us. They are not humans. They are wild creatures. And it would be a mistake to think they are the same as us."

"Mistake?"

"The sea has a soul but no compassion," said Gamle Jenny solemnly.

"What does that mean?"

"It means that a havfrue only befriends a human when she wants them to join her in the deep."

"The deep? But Lorelei knows I couldn't breathe underwater!" Freya said, shocked.

"Yes," replied Gamle Jenny calmly, giving Freya a kind look. "Perhaps it is their way of showing friendship, I do not know. But the danger to you is clear.

You cannot trust Lorelei, no matter how friendly she seems. Her world is not your world."

Freya remembered all the stories she'd heard about havfrue snatching babies and eating them. She shuddered.

"You don't think…they eat babies do you?"

"No," Gamle Jenny said, choosing her words carefully. "I don't believe they mean to hurt us. Those stories came about because silly parents did not supervise their children near the water's edge. When a toddler drowns parents look for something to blame, anything but themselves."

"That's really sad." Freya put down her bottle. Staring out the window she thought of Lorelei, gliding through the emerald green water, down to the unknown depths to a cave, alone. She turned to Gamle Jenny. "I think Lorelei is lonely," she said. "I think she needs me as a friend. And I trust her."

Gamle Jenny pursed her lips. "The sea has a soul but no compassion," she repeated. "Be careful, little one. Remember what I said. Stay on the rocks, but do not, I repeat, *do not go into the water*. It will only tempt your friend to take you."

"Is that why Mamma doesn't like me swimming by myself? Or even going out in Bestefar's boat?"

"Yes, of course. Your mother is trying to protect you."

Freya swallowed. "I see."

"Will you promise me not to go into the water?"

"I promise," Freya said gravely. "Even though I don't believe Lorelei would hurt me, I promise not to go into the water." There was a strangeness about the havfrue that had convinced Freya that Gamle Jenny was right. They were friends but they were from two different worlds. And Lorelei's world was too dangerous for Freya. She recalled the accident the other day when she had fallen out of the boat and almost drowned. The terror of salty water being sucked into her lungs. The helpless thrashing around, with no one there to help. The cold numbness in her limbs. No, it was Lorelei's world but not hers.

"Did you guess about Lorelei?" Freya asked, fingering her pendant. "Did you see her talking to me?"

Gamle Jenny smiled wistfully. "I didn't see your Lorelei, but when I was about your age I was sure I saw a flash of tail out in the middle of Stranda fjord. There is magic in the deep, Freya. Old, old magic. Mørke engler prowl about, swimming with the seals and the fish. Wild and strange."

"Lorelei isn't a mørk engel!" Freya cried.

"Hush, child, I believe you. But just remember that the legends have a grain of truth."

Freya gasped. "Do you think Lorelei is in danger from them?"

Gamle Jenny leaned back in her chair.

"No. I think she has survived quite well up until now. She is probably fierce enough to manage herself."

Freya smiled. "Yes. She's very strong. I'm sure she's all right." She glanced at her watch. "I'd better be going, before Mamma starts worrying. It's breakfast time."

Gamle Jenny got to her feet slowly and awkwardly. Freya helped her.

"Shall I wrap the rest of the cake for you?"

"Yes please!"

"Come into the kitchen then, Freya."

As Freya set off for her house she felt so happy she had confided in Gamle Jenny. It had been the right decision. And tomorrow she would tell Lorelei all about it.

CHAPTER EIGHT

When Freya arrived home with the cake everyone had finished breakfast.

"Where have you been lille venn?" Asked Mamma, stacking dishes in the sink and turning on the water. "I made scrambled eggs with cheese on top – your favourite. What do you have there?"

"I went to see Gamle Jenny and she gave me this chocolate cake for my birthday! She said her daughter Anna was visiting yesterday so she couldn't come over." Freya put the cake down on the table and lifted the pendant between her fingers to show her mother. "And she gave me this havfrue pendant. Isn't it beautiful?"

Mamma touched the pendant with her fingertip and nodded. "Yes, very sweet indeed. Aren't you a lucky girl? Now, what will you have for breakfast?" She wagged a finger. "And I don't mean chocolate cake."

"I'll just have cornflakes," said Freya, going over to the cupboard. "Where's Lisbet?"

"She hasn't come down yet," Mamma said, getting on with the dishes.

"Is Tante Nina coming over?"

"She's not feeling well so she stayed at home."

"Are you going to visit her later? Can I come?" Freya asked.

Mamma wiped her hands on a tea towel. "I'll go over after lunch. Of course you can come."

"Is Lisbet is sick too?" Freya said.

Mamma looked out the window facing the big red barn, her eyes worried.

Freya frowned. "She's been so horrible to me lately Mamma. I don't understand what I've done."

Mamma came over to sit beside Freya. She gently rubbed circles on Freya's back.

"I really don't think it's anything you've done, my little good heart. Lisbet is going through something. And until she is ready to tell us we can't do much to help her."

"But why doesn't she even tell you? I would. I even told you about Lorelei, even though I know you don't really believe it. But you're happy for me to believe it, right?"

Mamma smiled. "I would never crush your childhood dreams, vennen min. If you believe Lorelei is real then she is real. But beware," Mamma added solemnly. "The sea has a soul but no compassion."

"That's exactly what Gamle Jenny said," Freya replied indignantly.

"Do you understand what it means?" Mamma asked gently.

"That Lorelei wants me to come and live in the deep with her. But I don't believe that. Lorelei is kind and understanding and she listens to me. She'd never do anything to hurt me."

"Not intentionally. Just promise me you'll be careful."

"I promised you I wouldn't go into the water, Mamma. And I won't. But please don't stop me from seeing Lorelei."

"I trust you, Freya, to keep your word. And that is enough for me."

Freya gently removed the cling wrap from the cake and cut a generous slice, placing it on a small side plate.

"I'm going to take this up to Lisbet. Perhaps the sister I used to know is hiding there inside her and will come out when she sees this magnificent slice of chocolate cake I'm sharing with her! Even if she's forgotten how to be a good sister, I haven't."

"An excellent idea."

"And then I'm going to stay upstairs and do some colouring-in for a while." Freya climbed the stairs carefully balancing the plate. Gently she knocked on Lisbet's door. The voice from within was muffled. She knocked again.

"What do you want?" Demanded Lisbet angrily.

"I've brought you some of my chocolate cake Gamle Jenny made for my birthday. I thought this might cheer you up a bit. I don't have to come in. I'll just leave it outside your door okay?" There was no reply. Freya went to her own room, got out her colouring books, pencils and paints and spread them all over the floor. She'd only just begun to draw an outline of a havfrue when there was a knock on her open door. Lisbet stood there holding the empty plate.

"Thanks," she said.

"You look so sad, Lisbet. What's wrong?"

Lisbet's bottom lip trembled. She bit down hard on it.

"You can sit on my bed if you want," Freya suggested. Lisbet sat down, looking uncomfortable. Freya decided to stay on the floor. "Guess what? Lorelei is real. I know you think it was a big joke to convince me to go down to the water so early in the morning, but it's true! And now she's my friend. I've been chatting to her every day."

Lisbet's big sad eyes filled with tears and she buried her face in her hands, her shoulders heaving. Freya passed her the pillow. Her sister sobbed into it, while Freya sat beside her and stroked her back. After a while Lisbet's sobs subsided. Staring out the small attic window she said quietly, "I hate this place. I just want to leave. But where would I go? It's like a prison here. A cold, dark, stinky prison with no escape."

Freya stared at her sister, as if she were a stranger.

"How can you hate this beautiful place?" Freya said incredulously. "Think of all the times we rode around the island on our bikes collecting hazelnuts and went blueberry picking with our family in the blueberry forest. And in summertime last year when we made that amazing raft. And in winter when you skied down the slope and did that magnificent curve right at the end. And the view over the water on a calm day or a stormy day. How can you hate this place?"

Lisbet turned a fierce face towards her younger sister, her white gold hair in disarray around her face. "What do you know? You're too little to understand! This place is hell for me! And I just want to run away!" She threw down the pillow and ran from the room.

CHAPTER NINE

When Lisbet didn't come down for lunch Mamma covered a plateful of food with cling wrap and put it in the fridge for later. Then she and Freya set off with a basket of fresh bread rolls to see Tante Nina.

Onkel Felix and Tante Nina's house was painted Norwegian blue with white window frames and sat on a slight rise looking out over the fjord. The dairy was situated halfway between the houses of the two brothers. The family shared many meals together, as was the Askvold family tradition begun by Freya's grandparents Petter and Hilde Askvold. 'Family comes first' was their motto and although Freya's memories of Bestemor and Bestefar were few and faded, the motto rang true every day. Family was the only thing that mattered, but sometimes family was the reason they fought, too. As

Freya walked along the path through the pine trees holding Mamma's hand she thought that her uncle and her father, as brothers, were sometimes just as touchy with each other, as Lisbet and herself. And yet the brothers often had fun too, despite working every day together in their family business.

It was difficult, dirty work, and there was no holiday from it because who would want to fill in, getting up at five am to milk cows? Despite modern equipment in *fjøset,* (the barn), so many things could go wrong. Many times Freya had seen the suction caps fall off, or when mastitis hadn't been detected soon enough and the machine had sucked blood into the vat, contaminating the milk. Though the black and white Friesian cows were fairly even-tempered, with their big, doleful brown eyes, they were very large beasts with a powerful kick that could break your leg or send you flying across the dairy, onto the concrete, slick with watery, stinky manure. Sometimes they would refuse to go into the stall and it would take both men, struggling with ropes and hands to get them in. Freya had wanted to name all the cows because she felt sorry for them. But Pappa had said number tags in their ears were perfectly adequate and that she shouldn't become too attached.

Their calves were taken away at an early age and the sound of their distressed calling could last for days and days, haunting Freya's dreams at night. But in order to have milk to sell, cows had to give birth every year and every year have their babies taken from them after the first week. The only enjoyment for Freya was helping to hand feed the calves, as they stood on their wobbly legs in their stalls. She would always take extra straw to make it snug for them, the poor babies, who she was certain missed snuggling up to their mums. It was fun to teach them how to suck milk from the bucket. First you allowed them to suck your fingers and then gradually placed your hand inside the bucket where they started to suck the milk. There was often coughing and spluttering which could be quite comical, but when they were hungry the calves learned very quickly. Only the very small, sickly calves were bottle-fed and if they didn't thrive within a few days they mysteriously disappeared. Freya never asked where they went. She tried not to imagine it either. Life on a farm could be harsh that way. But only the strong could survive and for a family business that was absolutely necessary. Weak calves would mean weak cows, who could not be relied upon to provide regular milk, who might even spread sickness to others or give birth to sickly calves. When she was nine Freya had become very attached to a little bull calf she called Frankie and when he failed to thrive she had passionately fought to have him buried in the garden, where she'd made a little headstone for him. She painted one of the smooth grey rocks from the shore with some white house paint. The headstone read: *Frankie – a little fighter*. She knew she had done everything to help Frankie survive, but sometimes nature was cruel and had other ideas.

Tante Nina opened the door looking like a pale waif in her light pink hoody and matching track pants. The fluffy pale blue slippers added to the fragility of her appearance. There were dark rings under her eyes and her normally sleek, soft golden hair was tied back roughly in an untidy bun, looking dull and listless. She smiled weakly and ushered them inside. The house smelled stale, as if it hadn't been aired for days. Mamma went straight to the kitchen and began tidying up and cleaning, despite Tante Nina's protests. Mamma became brisk.

"Nina, go and sit with Freya. Tell her stories from when you were a girl. I know she would love to hear them."

"Yes, Tante Nina!" cried Freya eagerly. "Tell me your stories. I've hardly heard anything, except the one about strawberry picking with your family that time when you ate too many and threw up in the car." Freya giggled.

Tante Nina looked like she was about to vomit right now. Her hand flew to her mouth.

"Just a minute," she said and fled to the bathroom.

Freya looked at her mother through the kitchen doorway. "Oops."

"It's all right, Freya. She'll be back in a minute."

While she waited, Freya got up and wandered over to the wall shelves to look at all the wooden carvings that Onkel Felix had made. Standing ten centimetres tall they were deftly carved with life-like precision depicting animals and birds of the forest and sea. Freya touched each one with her finger tip, marvelling at the movement her uncle managed to create in wood. Birds with their wings outstretched looked as if they were ruffling them right now. A little fox looked up as if he'd just heard the sound of his prey. A fish arched and seemed to leap out from the water for sheer joy. Onkel Felix often sat with a small block of wood and a sharp knife while the rest of the family watched television or chatted after dinner. He had once said that keeping his hands busy kept his mind from the pain in his leg.

Tante Nina returned and when they had settled on the sofa, she leafed through a photo album that had been handed down to Tante Nina by her mother. It contained many precious photographs of her ancestors and her immediate family. Tante Nina's brother, Kenneth, had died as a boy of six. But she, being the elder sister, had very vivid memories of her little brother and talked about him joyfully.

"He was such a little tease!" She said with a wry smile. "He'd sneak up behind me and put things in my underpants. Imagine that!"

"What?" Freya cried, horrified, imagining Lisbet doing that to her. "What sorts of things?"

"Oh, frogs, crickets, any sort of bug he could get his little hands on."

Freya squirmed and shuddered.

"I'm glad Lisbet doesn't do that to me."

"He was such a dear little boy," Tante Nina said sadly. "I miss him."

"Where is his grave?" Asked Freya.

"On the mainland," replied Tante Nina. "I do visit him sometimes when I'm over there. Usually when I'm by myself, as your uncle isn't keen to go to the cemetery."

"Why does he hate that place so much?"

"I'm not really sure," Tante Nina said evasively. She squeezed Freya's hand. "You just want everyone to be happy, don't you, Freya? But there are some things we cannot change." She looked up and her gaze met that of her sister-in-law. Another look passed between them which Freya could not interpret. What was this secret language the two women shared? It was a mystery.

"Here's me at my confirmation," Tante Nina's beautifully manicured finger pointed at a black-and-white photo of a young girl in a pretty white dress holding a small posy of flowers. "It will be your turn soon. Do you have a dress picked out?"

"Mamma says I have to use Lisbet's," Freya said, feeling resentful. She didn't want to wear Lisbet's hand-me-down, even if the dress had only been worn once. She knew for a fact there was a small oil stain right on the front which Mamma had scrubbed and scrubbed without success. And she knew every child in her confirmation class would notice and laugh at her.

"How would you like to borrow this one?" Tante Nina said, pointing to the dress she had worn.

Freya's heart skipped a beat. "Really? You'd let me borrow your precious dress? It's so beautiful, Tante Nina. I would hate to ruin it."

"Well I have no need for it, do I? And as I don't have any children..."

"But you're still young! You could still have babies," Freya reassured her. Tante Nina wiped her nose delicately, her eyes sad.

"We've tried for many years. It's just not meant to be."

Freya patted her aunt's hand. "You never know!" she said with a wink. "When you get better, you could..."

"Freya, would you come and help me with the tea please?" Mamma called from the kitchen. "Let Tante Nina put her feet up and rest."

The phone rang just as Freya walked past it.

"Hello, Askvold's house, this is Freya speaking."

"Good afternoon, this is Sergeant Nilson at Elveby police station. I am trying to locate Mrs Gretchen Askvold."

"Oh, yes, hold on. I'll fetch her for you." Freya held out the phone to her mother. "It's for you Mamma."

"For me? Who is it?"

"It's Elveby police." She watched as her mother listened to the police officer.

"She what? When? I see. Yes. Thank you for calling. We will arrange everything. Sorry to cause you trouble."

Freya was bursting to know. "What is it Mamma? What's happened?"

"Lisbet has run away. To the mainland." Mamma looked at Tante Nina. "She's at a friend's house. She made the friend swear not to tell us where she was, but the girl's mother thought it odd, so she rang our home. Of course there was no one there, so she rang the police."

"Why would Lisbet run away?" asked Tante Nina, her eyes wide with concern.

Mamma shook her head.

"I don't know. She won't speak to me."

"Or me," piped up Freya. "I gave her some of my chocolate cake and she burst into tears, sitting on my bed. I thought she would tell me what's wrong after that, but she just left."

"I wish I knew what was troubling her," Mamma whispered, staring at her hands.

"Gretchen, it's probably just a teenage love crush gone wrong. You remember what that was like, don't you? At the time it feels like the worst tragedy in the whole of human suffering," Tante Nina said with a wry smile. "But we got over it. And Lisbet will too."

Looking at her aunt's cheerful face Freya knew in her heart that this wasn't going to be true for her sister. The anger inside Lisbet's heart was powerful, greater than any love crush disappointment. It raged like a fire that could not be quenched.

CHAPTER TEN

Tante Nina had sent Freya to bed, but she heard her parents and sister arrive home late that night. No one said a word. When Pappa went quiet, you knew you'd really done something terrible and consequences were to follow. Freya wondered what punishment Lisbet would get for running away. She heard her sister's feet scuff on the wooden stairs. Freya got out of bed and opened her bedroom door just a crack. Lisbet was dressed in jeans and a black jacket Freya had never seen before, a red rucksack on her back. She moved slowly, as if in a trance, quietly closing her bedroom door behind her. It looked to Freya as if her sister's spirit was broken.

Lisbet didn't come down to breakfast next morning. Mamma took a tray up to her, although Pappa had insisted Lisbet come down and eat with the family. Mamma didn't argue, she just quietly arranged things on a tray and took them upstairs. Freya ate her toast with *brunost*, brown goat's cheese. When she'd finished she got up, filled the kettle and put it on to boil. Pappa liked his morning coffee and she felt very grown up being able to make one for him.

"Thank you Freya," said Pappa, smiling. He gave the newspaper a gentle shake and turned the page.

Freya poured hot water into the mug and stirred in some instant coffee, then added milk and sugar before placing the steaming cup in front of her father on the table.

"Pappa, what's wrong with Lisbet?"

"We're not sure, lille venn," Pappa said from within the folds of his paper. "Your mother has made an appointment on the mainland, so we'll be taking your sister there this week."

"Taking her where? Is it a doctor? What's wrong with her?"

"Now Freya," Pappa said firmly, folding his newspaper and taking a sip of his coffee. "I know you're worried about your sister, but this is adult business and big sister business. You are not to question her about it. Understand? It will only make things more difficult for her."

"But, Pappa…"

"Promise me, Freya, that you will leave your sister alone."

Freya bowed her head.

"Yes, Pappa."

"You get ready for school now."

Freya's head snapped up.

"What about Lisbet?"

"She won't be going to school today. Mamma will give you a note for the teacher."

As Freya walked to the bus stop alone through the pine trees, hearing them gently sigh in the breeze, she felt that the island itself was sad for Lisbet. Even the seagulls sounded more mournful than usual. As she waited for the minibus, sitting alone in the old milk churn shed, she watched the curly white clouds scuttling across the deep blue sky. She wished she could fly up there with the Canadian geese who had begun arriving with the onset of spring. The large wild geese were easily identifiable with their black head and neck, white cheeks, white strap under the chin and a brown body. Their cries as they flew overhead seemed friendly to Freya, as if they were saying, 'Thank goodness it's spring again! We love coming here.'

The school day seemed to drag on and on. Freya's teacher, Mrs Lindstrøm, was a young woman with short dark hair and a wiry build. She was very quick in her movements, darting from one side of the room to the other, keeping track of everyone, including the naughty boys in the class, Nils and Rune. Freya especially enjoyed Art and story time, although today there wasn't enough time to finish the story that she'd started writing. So she shoved the sheets of paper into her schoolbag, meaning to finish it at home. It was a story of two sisters who lived on an island and one of the sisters had a terrible secret. She called the sisters Mia and Lise.

Normally Freya sat next to Britt, whose parents also ran a dairy, on the mainland, but Britt was absent from school today, so there was no one to talk to at recess or lunch. Freya found a bench apart from everyone else and sat by herself to eat. Some of the girls walked past in a group, arms linked and laughing.

Freya ran from the bus stop down towards Gamle Jenny's house, panting all the way, then jogged breathlessly through the pine trees and to the open hillside. Heaving open the back door she raced upstairs to change. Lisbet's door remained closed. Without even bothering to get herself a snack, Freya ran down the grassy slope to the spot where she had called Lorelei.

Today it seemed to take a bit longer for the havfrue to hear her and Freya wondered if it had all been her imagination. But then, she heard a splash and saw Lorelei's beautiful frilly tail slap the water. Shortly afterwards the havfrue emerged, glistening and lovely, to sit herself on her usual rock and regard Freya with her usual expression.

"Lisbet ran away from home," Freya said, shaking her head. "I don't understand her at all. She says she hates this place, that it's like a prison. Why would you think that? This island," Freya flung her arms wide. "Is a paradise! And we are so lucky to live here. Don't you think?"

Lorelei double blinked, scratched at her pale green arm and rearranged her straw-like hair to dry in the sun. A crab clung to the strands of her hair and she delicately released it before shoving it in her mouth and crunching noisily. Freya stared in fascinated horror. She couldn't imagine eating a crab raw but havfrue were wild creatures, just as Gamle Jenny had said.

"Lisbet has an appointment in town this week. I reckon it's a doctor. Maybe she…" Freya shook her head. "No, there's no point trying to figure it out. They'll probably never tell me. Nobody tells me anything. Do you think I'm too young to understand?" She asked of her friend.

"Squawk!" Answered Lorelei, pointing out into the middle of the fjord.

Freya turned to stare in the direction Lorelei had pointed but she saw nothing. Perhaps a ripple on the surface, very slight.

"What is it? What do you see?" Freya asked, squinting.

Lorelei grunted, as if to say, *are your human eyes that weak?*

"Would you like me to bring you something tomorrow?" Freya asked. "Something different to eat? I still have some birthday cake left over. Would you like that?"

Lorelei opened her small mouth. Freya could clearly see the sharp pointed teeth, slightly yellowed around the gums. A piercing shriek erupted. She patted her flat, muscular chest with both hands and then reached out to Freya.

"What is it, Lorelei? What are you trying to tell me?" Freya asked.

Lorelei grunted, then preened her tail for a few seconds, nimbly picking out tiny bits of shell which she popped into her mouth and crunched. She scanned the water with her strange eyes, as if thinking.

"You're leaving, aren't you?" Freya said. Lorelei blinked at her, then in one fluid movement slipped off the rock and into the water, like she was made of it. Freya sat watching the fjord, listening to the delicious splashing around the small rocks and pebbles in the shallows. The tide was coming back in. It was time to go.

Freya did not see Lisbet at all that Monday. On Tuesday morning Mamma again took a tray upstairs while Pappa shook the newspaper and read out the football scores. Onkel Felix came in after the first milking for a coffee and then disappeared again. Tante Nina was still sick.

CHAPTER ELEVEN

Syttende Mai, the seventeenth of May, was tomorrow and Freya felt the usual flutter of excitement in her tummy. Syttende Mai was such an important day in the life of every Norwegian as it celebrated Constitution Day, Norway's independence from Sweden in 1814. On this special day, each year, every town celebrated with a parade through the main streets called a *torg*. Many organisations would take part, such as schools, firefighters, police, charities, brass bands and many more. The rest of the community would stand lining the streets to clap and cheer and wave Norwegian flags as the torg went by. Everywhere the red, white and blue of the Norwegian flag, in streamers, ribbons and rosettes, decorated homes, buildings, even children's prams. At school in Elveby Freya's class had been making decorations for weeks.

Food was also a big part of Syttende Mai celebrations and Mamma never disappointed with her delicious offerings. Freya's favourite was *kransekake,* a very special cake, a tower of eight sweet almond rings stacked on top of one another with a tiny Norwegian flag perched on top. Kransekake was deliciously chewy, crisp on the outside, drizzled with lemony icing, which was Mamma's personal touch to this traditional cake. If she could, Freya would have eaten kransekake every day. Syttende Mai was a family day, when grown children would return to their home town to catch up with old friends and stay with their family.

On Eikeberg Island there was the usual torg, on the main road, beginning at the standing stone memorial to King Håkon Herdebrei, past the church at the top of the hill, down into a shallow valley, past the school and museum, following the bus route and down past the driveway of the Askvold family and ending at the home of a famous lady poet, Synnøve Sigurdson, who had once lived on Eikeberg.

Everyone who was able, who could afford it, would wear their national dress costume. These traditional costumes were brightly coloured, made of soft, felted wool fabric and based on the style of formal dress in the 1800's, the time when Norway became an independent nation. Traditionally they would be handmade and embroidered, each region having its own special styles, colours and motifs. The women wore a crisp white blouse with a beautiful silver brooch at their throat underneath their *bunad,* (national dress costume) which was like an over-dress, fitted to the waist and then flared to almost floor length. A small, embroidered purse in the same fabric and design would hang from the belt of the dress. Special black shoes, with large ornate buckles, stepped out of history on that day, as the style of shoe hadn't changed for hundreds of years. The men wore three quarter felted trousers, a white shirt and waistcoat, sometimes with a jacket and even a top hat. It was a proud day for Norwegians, a day of celebrating their special history. One of the more unusual groups to participate in the torg were the high school students who were in their last year of schooling. Traditionally they wore red overalls. It was a great honour to be in this group, marching through the town. Stories from all over the country that day would be shared on the TV news throughout the day and evening.

Mamma was of course German, so she was not permitted to wear a bunad, but Tante Nina wore hers proudly, which had been handmade and embroidered by her grandmother and passed down through her mother to her. Pappa and Onkel Felix would be wearing identical outfits of their region.

The smells of baking in the kitchen were almost unbearable to Freya, as she walked through to the back door. Mamma's apron was covered in flour and there was a smudge of white on her cheek. Her sleeves were rolled up and her face was slightly flushed from kneading the almond dough.

"Where are you off to, lille venn?"

"I'm just going down to see Lorelei. I wonder if she knows about Syttende Mai?"

"I'm sure your friend knows," said Mamma, puffing. "Havfruer are often hundreds of years old, aren't they?"

"You mean you believe in her?" Freya asked joyfully.

Mamma turned, wiping her hands on her apron and gave Freya a smile.

"It doesn't matter what I believe, vennen min. It's what you believe that counts. And if Lorelei is a good friend to you, then you are very fortunate."

"I wish Lisbet could be friends with her too," said Freya, hanging her head. "Mamma, she seems so sad. What's wrong with my big sister?"

Mamma's smile dropped from her face. She opened her arms and Freya nestled into her mother's embrace.

"I wish I could say, lille venn."

"Doesn't that doctor know?"

"Sometimes these things take time to figure out," said Mamma, stroking Freya's hair.

By the time the afternoon milking was done and Pappa came into the kitchen around five, the large room was hung with national costumes which had been aired and steamed. Mamma sat at the kitchen table sipping a cup of tea and reading a book, surrounded by a colourful gallery of black, red, white, green and royal blue. Freya's fingers caressed the hem of her own bunad, the thick, woollen fabric. Lisbet and Freya both had the Stranda and Elveby bunads – red bodice, royal blue skirt - which Mamma herself had made. Freya wore Lisbet's hand-me-down, a simpler version of the adult bunad. It had the hem taken up and the bodice taken in. Tante Nina had embroidered the matching purses for both girls as a Christmas gift. Lisbet's brand new beautifully embroidered bunad had been gifted to her on her sixteenth birthday. As was tradition, it was to last her for her lifetime. Bunads cost a great deal of money and when not used for special occasions such as Syttende Mai, weddings, funerals and other celebration days, they were carefully stored flat between layers of tissue paper and dried lavender in the large trunk in the attic.

"Mamma, do you think Tante Nina will be well enough tomorrow?" Freya asked.

"I hope so. Make sure you wash your hair tonight, Freya. I want you looking your best tomorrow."

Freya nodded and sat beside her mother.

"I wish you could wear a bunad, Mamma. It doesn't seem fair, just because you weren't born here."

Mamma put down her cup. "You must remember that people's memories are long, Freya," she said. "During the war, under German rule, no one was allowed to wear the bunad or celebrate Syttende Mai at all."

"But that wasn't your idea!" Freya cried passionately, her fingers squeezing Mamma's arm. "You weren't even born then!"

Mamma smiled wistfully. "Well, perhaps I could wear national dress from my own country," she said.

"That's a fantastic idea! But what would it look like?"

"Well, first I would have to decide if I choose the German national dress of my birthplace or the Austrian national dress where my family now lives," said Mamma. She turned back to her book. "Maybe next year, knuppen. We'll see."

Freya got up and skipped to the door then turned. "Well I'm going to write a story about it, right now," she said and ran to the stairs.

As the family sat down to dinner that evening, with a pale faced Lisbet picking at a small portion of food on her plate, it seemed no one but Freya was excited about the next day. Very soon she realised her eager babbling was being met with silence from her parents and grumpy sighs from her sister, so she fell silent, staring at each forkful of cheesy macaroni as she ate.

There was a knock on the back door. Freya's fork clattered to her plate as she shot to her feet.

"I'll get it!"

She wrenched open the door and there stood a tall man who looked vaguely familiar.

"Hello there, young lady. You must be Freya." The man dropped to his haunches and extended his hand solemnly. "I'm very pleased to meet you. The last time I saw you, you were a tiny baby."

"Stefan! Come in," said Mamma with a broad smile. Pappa pulled out the chair closest.

"*Velkommen*, (welcome) little brother," Pappa said. "You didn't tell us you were coming!"

In walked the strange but familiar man with wavy blonde hair, warm brown eyes and attractive face. He hugged his sister-in-law and brother before seating himself at the table. Grinning at Lisbet he exclaimed, "And Lisbet, you have grown into a young woman already. Why, you were four years old when I saw you last."

Lisbet said nothing just stared at her uncle as if he were the most boring thing she had seen all day.

"Have you eaten?" Asked Mamma, getting up to fetch a plate and cutlery.

Onkel Stefan held up his hands. "I admit, I had a sandwich at the train station about three hours ago but I was saving myself for your delicious cooking, Gretchen."

"What brings you here?" Pappa asked.

"Can't a man visit his family without being quizzed?" Said Onkel Stefan with a chuckle. Mamma and Pappa exchanged looks. Again, looks which Freya could not interpret.

"Where do you live, Onkel Stefan?" Asked Freya. "Is it nice there? Is it warmer than here? Is it on an island? Are you married?"

"Wow, little one, your brain works so fast! Which one of those hundred questions would you like me to answer first?"

Freya laughed. He had only been here a few minutes but already she liked Onkel Stefan very much.

In the morning when Freya opened her bedroom door she saw that Onkel Stefan was still asleep on the guest bed in one of the larger bedrooms upstairs. She tried to sneak past without waking him but the floorboards creaked. She froze, hoping he hadn't heard and stared at him. He looked similar to her father and Onkel Felix, the same square chin, strong nose and deep-set eyes, but his colouring was very different from her brown haired father and very dark featured Onkel Felix. Onkel Stefan's colouring could best be described as sandy. Even though he was the youngest of the three brothers he was definitely the tallest, with a slim build. He moved very differently to Onkel Felix, whose bad leg made him lean side to side as he walked. Onkel Stefan had lifted her high into the air last night when he'd said good night, making her shriek with joy and excitement.

Pappa hadn't lifted her since she was about five years old.

"It's all right, Freya. I am already awake," said Onkel Stefan, sitting up and rubbing his eyes. He wore a pair of Pappa's striped pyjamas. He patted the bed. "Come and sit here and tell me all about school."

Freya sat gingerly on the edge of the bed. Onkel Stefan smelled of pleasant cologne. His clean-shaven face had barely any bristles, unlike her father whose face was rough first thing in the morning and who loved to make her squeal by rubbing his chin on her neck.

"Well, my teacher is Mrs Lindstrøm."

"Is she nice? Does she spank the naughty boys?" Onkel Stefan chuckled.

Freya snorted. "I wish she did! Nils and Rune are a pain in the neck, especially when I am trying to concentrate on writing my stories or drawing a picture. And they are always teasing the girls. Although some of the girls seem to like it. But I definitely don't. They're a nuisance."

Onkel Stefan tipped back his head and roared with laughter. "So you're not rushing off to get married to one of them anytime soon then?"

"What?" Freya exclaimed in horror. "Do you mean that?"

"Of course not! Vennen min, it was just my little joke."

"Are you married?"

For the first time since he had arrived, Onkel Stefan was quiet.

"Are you...did you get a divorce?" Freya asked, searching his face anxiously.

"That's a bit personal, don't you think?" Demanded Lisbet, standing in the doorway, the perpetual frown on her face. "Wait until I tell Mamma how rude you are."

"It's all right," Onkel Stefan said, holding up his hand to forestall Lisbet's objection.

"I didn't mean to be rude!" Freya cried. "Why are you so mean to me, Lisbet? Haven't you got anything better to do than think up ways to hurt my feelings?"

"You're such a baby, Freya," replied Lisbet stiffly and walked away.

"See what I have to put up with?" Freya said under her breath.

"You should try having two older brothers," said Onkel Stefan, meaningfully. "You can never do anything right."

Freya's eyes widened. "Yes! That's exactly what it's like!"

"Well, I suppose I had better get up," said her uncle, pulling back the covers." See you at breakfast?"

Freya hopped off the bed. "Yep! See you down there."

Mamma was already up and had set the table with delicious breakfast things they didn't normally have, such as home-made strawberry jam, fresh potato pancakes, three types of cheese and kaviar, (fish roe paste with mayonnaise in a tube), which was Pappa's favourite. Breakfast was a more noisy and joyful affair than it had been for a very long time. Onkel Stefan had so many funny stories and seemed to draw even Lisbet out of her shell a little. He laughed a lot, did Onkel Stefan. And Freya wished with all her heart that he lived on the island too, so that she could see him more often.

"Where's Felix?" Asked Stefan.

"He'll be round soon to say hello," said Pappa, biting into his toast and kaviar paste. "I told him you were here."

"And I'm hoping Tante Nina is well enough to wear her beautiful bunad today," said Freya. "You should see it! It's stunning. Her grandmother hand stitched every single flower."

"I'm sure it's going to look wonderful," said Onkel Stefan, smiling across at her.

They just finished packing up the breakfast things and were doing the dishes when the back door opened and Onkel Felix walked in looking grim, as usual, followed by Tante Nina, who looked pale as had become the norm for her lately.

"Hello, Nina," said Onkel Stefan warmly, giving her a hug. Tante Nina seemed to perk up a little as she smiled up at her brother-in-law.

"Stefan, how lovely to see you! You'll have to forgive my appearance, I haven't been very well lately." She said smoothing her hair, looking embarrassed.

Onkel Stefan gently picked up her hand and kissed it gallantly.

"You look lovely as ever, dear sister-in-law."

Freya smiled. And then she saw Onkel Felix's face. He looked like he was holding in dark, boiling anger.

"Come on, Nina," he said briskly. "We've said hello now it's time to go home and get ready."

"Aren't you staying for a cup of tea?" Asked Mamma.

"No time for that," said Onkel Felix, his dark brows drawn together, avoiding looking at his youngest brother.

"Perhaps later today," said Tante Nina. Her face lit up again as she smiled at Onkel Stefan. "We'll see you in town?"

"Of course," he replied. "Wouldn't miss it. And Freya tells me you look stunning in your bunad."

Tante Nina blushed. "I don't know about that. I'll do my best." She smiled.

As the back door closed behind them, Freya felt Tante Nina looked a little better this morning. A little happier, perhaps. Onkel Stefan seemed to have that effect on everyone. Everyone, that is, except for his brother Felix.

CHAPTER TWELVE

Syttende Mai morning was sunny and crisp as the family stepped out from the kitchen porch at eight o'clock. Joy glistened on every blade of grass. To Freya the blue sky over Strandafjord was a dome of happiness and hope. The green tang of the sea blew gently across the land and with it the memories of island dwellers over thousands of years. Seagulls preened themselves on the smooth grey rocks down by the shore. Freya watched a hawk fly over them with a squirming fish in its beak. She smiled, feeling a warmth in her belly, like Mamma's lamb stew on a cold winter's night. It was a perfect day. She wondered what Lorelei was doing right now and imagined her gliding through the emerald waters, hair streaming behind her, clutching a fish in her long fingers.

Freya and her family looked resplendent in their

traditional outfits. Onkel Stefan, who'd brought only a small suitcase, wore one of Pappa's suits. Lisbet had tried to stay behind, holed up in her room, but Pappa had insisted she join the family and after ten minutes quiet talking behind the closed bedroom door with Mamma, Lisbet had emerged dressed ready to go, her face pale and angry. Onkel Stefan had tried to cheer her but his efforts were met with a scowl.

They all walked together through the pine trees to Gamle Jenny's house where Pappa knocked on the door. Gamle Jenny opened it straight away, dressed in her finery. She was born in Bergen, a coastal city to the south. Her bunad was a lovely creamy white skirt and bodice, with simple red, gold and green flowers swirling over the bottom half, with a matching embroidered shawl and white shoes. With her wavy white hair, she looked like a snow queen. The mood lifted. Freya sighed. They all walked on to Onkel Felix and Tante Nina's house.

Onkel Felix answered the door dressed in an identical outfit to Pappa - black three quarter length wool pants with buttons up the side of the knee, long white socks, black shoes with the large pewter buckles and a white shirt under a green and red tartan waistcoat.

"She's ready," he assured them grimly, then called over his shoulder, "Come on woman! Everyone is waiting for you."

"It's all right brother," soothed Onkel Stefan smilingly. "We can wait." He received only a scowl in reply. Mamma shuffled her feet and looked out over the garden. Pappa cleared his throat. Freya watched the adult faces and felt a sorrow creeping in, despite the bright day. What was the matter with them all?

Then Tante Nina appeared. Her bunad was from the Stranda and Elveby region, like Lisbet's - a red fitted wool bodice, panels embroidered with flowing tendrils of pastel coloured flowers. She wore it over a white blouse with elegant sleeves, a large silver brooch pinned in the centre at her throat and a royal blue wool skirt whose hem was decorated with the same delicate flowers. Over her blonde hair she wore a traditional soft matching red cap. Onkel Stefan whistled in amazement. Onkel Felix scowled.

Papa said, "Good morning, Nina! Freya was right, you do look stunning."

"Yes, you look better already," agreed Mamma, taking her hand and squeezing it.

"Tante Nina, you look like a movie star!" Said Freya, hugging her. Her aunt smiled, her eyes sparkling like they hadn't for months.

"Right, let's go then," grumbled Onkel Felix, shifting his bad hip awkwardly to close the front door. He inclined his head at Gamle Jenny. "Morning Jenny."

"How lovely to see you both," the old lady said, receiving a light kiss on her cheek from Tante Nina.

The group walked up to the road, turned right and headed up past the school, the church and to the top of Monument Hill where over two hundred people were gathered, like a large flock of colourful, noisy birds. Brass instruments blew odd sounds at each other, little children screamed and chased one another around the gathered adults. Eikeberg Skole had painted a wonderful banner this year made by the older students, showing the school with the mountains behind it and the sparkling fjord, with 'Eikeberg Skole' in large capitals. Every island child would take part today, even grumpy Lisbet. Next year would be her last year of high school, so she would join her friends in Elveby at the parade. For now she was one of five seniors on Eikeberg. Arne Albertson, an island boy her age, walked casually over to Lisbet.

"Hei," he said, smiling but looking a little embarrassed. Lisbet scowled but responded with a softer tone than expected.

"Hei." She smoothed the red bodice of her bunad.

"Nice bunad," he said, shifting his feet.

She looked at him, her eyes dark and dangerous.

"It's what we all have to wear, isn't it? This stupid costume."

Arne looked embarrassed. "Well, you look nice anyway. See you later maybe?"

Lisbet shook her head and glanced at her parents, who were chatting with friends.

"Have to go home and help out with the usual boring stuff."

"Oh." His eyes roamed over Lisbet's hair and face. He seemed reluctant to go. Freya liked Arne. He was one of the few island kids who never teased her. In some ways he was like a big brother, a protector of sorts, even though their paths didn't cross very frequently. Why was Lisbet being so rude to him?

"Hei Arne," Freya said, smiling. "You look nice today."

Arne looked down at Freya. He grinned and patted her head.

"Good to see you too, Freya. Perhaps you can convince your sister to come to *festen,* (the party), at the school?"

"Oh yes! We'd love to!"

"Freya! What do you…" Lisbet began angrily.

"I'm going to ask Mamma," Freya cried eagerly. She spun on her heel and ran to her parents.

"What's the point?" Lisbet called after her. But Freya had seen a glimmer of something happy in her sister's face. Maybe going to festen with Arne would help too. Lisbet actually liked Arne. It was obvious to anyone.

Mamma was surprised at Freya's request, given Lisbet's behaviour of late, but she was happy that the girls would be socialising with the island children. Pappa said it would be fine and stroked her hair. Freya ran back to Lisbet and Arne who were standing awkwardly.

"Mamma says it's okay!" Freya puffed.

"That's good!" Said Arne happily.

Lisbet scowled, looking down at Freya's shoes.

"You've got mud all over your shoes, Freya."

"Who cares?" Freya flung up her hands. "We get to go to festen! Aren't you happy about that?"

Lisbet stared past Arne, to the tall spire of the white wooden church behind him. She shrugged.

"I suppose."

Freya saw the disappointment in Arne's face and just wanted to kick her sister in the shins and wake her up. But before she could say anything he shrugged, gave Freya a wistful smile and turned to go.

"See you at festen!" Said Freya, beaming.

"See you there," he said quietly and walked away.

Turning to face her sister, Freya put her hands on her hips. "Lisbet, why are you so…"

And just then the band started up and everyone had

to rush to get into their positions. As the parade passed by, Freya's family shouted and waved Norwegian flags and clapped. Their faces were shiny with happiness and pride. Freya loved Syttende Mai so much. Sigrid walked beside her now, waving a flag and her brother Arvid walked on Freya's other side.

"How come you never get anything new?" asked Sigrid suddenly, looking at Freya's hand-me-down bunad from Lisbet.

"Lisbet's old bunad is just as good as new," Freya countered. "She only wore it for four years, once a year, that's four times. There's nothing wrong with it," Freya added stubbornly, knowing how long Mamma worked to make it fit. Freya looked at Sigrid's bunad, which was obviously new. "Besides, you don't have an older sister, so they always have to buy new for you," she finished triumphantly, knowing Sigrid wished she had a sister instead of Arvid. She could see her companion mulling over this comment in her mind, trying to figure out who actually had the upper hand now. Freya hugged the delicious feeling of victory to her itself. Sigrid wasn't that smart.

As the end of the torg passed, all the adults joined in so that the entire island community walked together on the road, down past the school and museum and headed for Synnøve Sigurdson's house – a three storey mustard yellow painted house with white window frames which stood proudly on the hillside to the right, its windows facing the fjord. A wide balcony spanned the width of the house. It had been a museum for many years, but eventually the poet's family decided to sell it. It was now owned by a businessman from Elveby who chose to celebrate Syttende Mai on the mainland. In years gone by, when it was a museum, the house had been opened to the public on this special day and Freya had loved walking through it looking at the beautiful old furniture, the tapestries on the wall and the handcarved items in pale beechwood so typical of Norwegian culture. But today the house sat silent and waiting, like an old monarch waiting for her subjects to appear.

In Oslo, the capital city of Norway, the torg would be enormous, with thousands of people taking part. The torg in Oslo would wind its way through the main streets to the palace, where the Royal family would stand on the palace balcony and wave to the crowds.

After lunch, Freya felt the need to rush down to the water and call Lorelei. She decided to take some kransekake, to give to her special friend. After changing into play clothes, she skipped joyfully to her special spot, on the large rock smoothed by the ocean and warmed by the sun. Freya began to sing, watching the water for any ripples, signs of her enigmatic friend, but after ten minutes of singing, when her voice began to crack, Freya realised that Lorelei was not coming today. She wondered if the havfrue was attending an underwater ceremony? Perhaps that's what havfrue did on Syttende Mai. She opened the serviette in her hand and ate the piece of kransekake she had saved for Lorelei. The breeze had stiffened and was a little chilly now. Freya wanted to stay, just in case Lorelei appeared, but she also did not want to miss festen. She walked slowly back up the slope, stopping every few steps to check that Lorelei wasn't sitting on her usual rock, preening her hair. The wind had whipped the water to little white waves, chasing each other to the shore, but no havfrue sat waiting.

CHAPTER THIRTEEN

Festen was held at Eikeberg Skole hall, which was also where they played sport, had exams, held community meetings, concerts, fundraisers, wedding receptions, funeral wakes and other occasions - whenever a large room was needed.

Mamma had insisted the girls take a jacket and a torch, as even though the sun set later at this time of year, the path beneath the pine trees was still fairly dark on the way home. As they walked up the road towards the school Lisbet was silent, head down, lost in her thoughts. She was wearing all dark clothing, as if she wanted to blend in with the shadows and not be seen. The only colour she wore was pink lipstick.

"Lisbet," Freya said quietly.

"What," Lisbet said with a flat, dull voice.

"Are you okay?"

"Fine."

"You don't seem fine," Freya ventured bravely. "You don't seem like your normal self at all."

"What would you know, Mamma's little baby?"

"I wish you wouldn't call me that! Just because you're angry at something, doesn't mean I should cop it. It's just not fair!"

"Then don't ask. Don't bother your little head with my problems," Lisbet said quietly.

"But you're my sister," Freya said gently, her feet scuffing gravel on the road. "My big sister. Of course I worry about you. You're normally the one who looks after me, but it feels like at the moment I should be looking after you."

Lisbet was silent. Freya sneaked a sideways look and saw her sister swallowing repeatedly and blinking her eyes.

"There's nothing you can do," Lisbet said softly. "It's too late anyway."

"What's too late?"

"I said there's nothing you can do!" said Lisbet hotly, her face red and her eyes shining with unshed tears. "Just stay out of it, okay?"

Freya felt the embarrassment trapped inside Lisbet. She felt something else too – shame. Lisbet was ashamed of something. What on earth could she have done?

By the time they arrived at school it was six thirty. The local folk band was playing and the games had already started. Hearing the music Freya rushed in through the doors, spotted Sigrid and Arvid and ran over to them. The next time she saw her sister was when she went to the toilet. On the way to the restrooms at the back of the hall she noticed Lisbet sitting in a corner by herself staring into a plastic cup dejectedly. She noticed Arne making his way over to Lisbet and hoped he would be able to cheer her sister up.

With a tummy full of sausage rolls, cake and *lefse,* (a rolled up pancake with cinnamon, butter and sugar), and a bottle of bright yellow Solo in her hand, Freya joined some of the island children outside to play a game of tag. Very soon she abandoned her drink and joined in, feeling for the first time, as if she were actually an accepted island child.

At eight thirty, the time Pappa had said they must start walking back, Freya went to find her sister. She saw Arne and asked him, but he just shrugged and said he hadn't seen Lisbet for over an hour.

"Is something going on with her?" Arne asked.

Freya shook her head. "I don't know. She won't talk to anyone about it."

"She's not herself," Arne commented.

Freya looked up into Arne's friendly face, his dark wavy hair and bright blue eyes. His nose was covered with tiny freckles that moved when he smiled. Of all the island boys he was the only one who seemed to care about the Askvold sisters.

"I wish you could help her," Freya said softly, feeling tears well up in her eyes. A hard lump was squashed in her throat and she tried to swallow it.

"I wish I could too," he said with a wistful smile. "Lisbet deserves to be happy, just like anyone else."

"She's never been like this before," said Freya, studying Arne's black suede lace up boots. "Anyway, I'd better find her because Pappa said we have to go home now."

"Want me to help you?" He said.

Freya searched the room one more time before answering.

"Yes, please."

"Did you check in the toilets?"

"Yes. She's not there." Freya said.

"All right then. Let's go." Arne took her hand and they walked outside together. It was so much easier having Arne there to help because he could go up to anyone and they would listen. But no one remembered seeing Lisbet at least for the last half-hour. As they stood around the back of the building, looking around, at each other questioningly, they heard someone sobbing. It was a very faint sound, as if it were coming from inside the building. Freya spun. Her feet were right outside one of the basement windows. She crouched down and peered inside, but the interior was too dark.

"I think Lisbet's in here!" She said to Arne. He frowned, then grabbed her hand and ran back inside. They had to fumble and find several light switches to get down to the basement. Freya was glad she had a torch with her, especially on the stairs. As they opened the door to a small storage room the sobbing ceased.

"Lisbet?" Freya called out. "Are you in here?" Silence greeted them. Arne switched on the light. There were boxes and mops and buckets and some old furniture but no sign of Lisbet.

"Lisbet?" Said Arne gently. "We heard you outside. I promise I won't ask what it is that's bothering you, but you need to come out now. Freya needs you to walk her home." For many long seconds there was only silence and then suddenly Lisbet appeared from behind some boxes in the corner. Her hair was dishevelled, her face red and puffy. Arne looked desolate at the sight of her. His arms came forward as if he were going to hug her but then fell limp against his sides again. Lisbet stared hard at him then swung her gaze upon Freya.

"Why did you bring him down here? I don't need anyone's help."

"Clearly," Arne said, his brow arched.

"Shut up!" Lisbet snarled. "Leave me alone, Arne."

Arne stood, watching her as she came forward, wiping her nose on her sleeve.

"Come on Freya, don't just stand there!" Lisbet snapped.

The sisters started off down the road together.

"Why on earth did you bring Arne into this?" Lisbet demanded angrily.

"Lisbet, I couldn't find you! What did you expect me to do? I'm only twelve. Arne was there and he asked me if I needed help, which I did, in case you didn't notice, because you decided to go and hide down in the basement!"

Lisbet stuck at her chin stubbornly.

"Where I go is no one else's business."

"Well, it was *my* business because we had to go home!" Freya retorted.

"When will you just leave me alone?" Lisbet hissed. "I don't need your help, little sister. You're seriously of no use to me." She sped up to a jog, leaving Freya running after her.

"Lisbet! Wait for me!"

By the time Freya pushed through the kitchen door she could hardly breathe. Mamma wiped her hands on a tea towel and rushed over to Freya, putting hands on her daughter's shoulders and searching her face.

"Freya! Why did you run? Now you're having an asthma attack!" Exclaimed Mamma worriedly.

Freya burst into tears. How could she explain the hurt she was feeling? How could she explain the worry about Lisbet, without giving that worry to her mother, who was already struggling to cope with Lisbet's moods? She clung to her mother, burying her face in Mamma's soft clothing. Soon the comforting smells of baking and Mamma's gentle perfume calmed her. She pulled away.

"I'm fine now. I suppose I should have a shower."

Mamma stroked her hair.

"If you're sure?"

Freya nodded, though her chest felt too tight for her breath.

"Yes. I'll be all right." From the adjoining lounge room Freya heard her father and Onkel Stefan laughing, but the sound gave her no comfort.

When she reached the attic, Freya heard Lisbet's loud music through her closed door. It was a harsh, angry noise, but wrapped inside it was the wretched sound of her sister's sobbing. As she lay her head on the pillow later that night, Freya decided to pray to God. She only ever prayed when the situation was extremely hopeless. She hadn't even prayed about Lorelei, because she had known in her heart that Lorelei was real. But this problem with Lisbet was a frightening mystery- a dark thing with, as yet, no name.

CHAPTER FOURTEEN

The next day at school Britt was still away. Freya felt more than just alone, she felt as if she were standing on the roof and everyone was staring up at her. Her sister's absence was a topic of gossip all day and some of the comments were very unkind. Freya didn't understand completely what the high school girls were saying but she could tell by the way they sniggered that they had no regard for Lisbet's feelings or what she was going through. And that made her mad. By the end of lunch her anger had reached boiling point and when she heard two girls talking by the bubblers she marched over and shouted at them.

"What do you know? You know nothing! My sister is so unhappy right now she just wants to run away and all you can do is make fun of her! What's wrong with you?" And then she stalked off without looking back.

Mrs Lindstrøm wasn't much help either. She was so busy organising a sports carnival and chatting to her favourite students – the sporty ones – that she failed to notice Freya's unhappiness, the dried tears on her cheek, the uneaten sandwich sitting on the corner of her desk. Mrs Lindstrøm was good at discipline but not much interested in any emotional problems her students had. Unless you were very good at sport, then she gave you her full attention. If you were the best skier, ice skater, ice hockey player, swimmer or baseball player you received lots of smiles and encouragement, but if you were just very good at reading and writing stories you were virtually invisible.

Freya missed Britt very much that day. Britt also loved reading, although her spelling was atrocious and she had trouble getting her ideas down on paper. But Britt lived on a dairy too and seemed to understand things about farm life that the other children didn't. And she wasn't ashamed to talk about feeding the calves or the muck you had to walk through in winter, coming almost up to the top of your gumboots as you helped your father muck out the stalls. In Norway the cows were kept indoors all through winter and this meant a lot of work and a lot of manure to remove. Sometimes Freya's efforts were rewarded when she searched among the hay bales for Snuppen, the brindle cat who lived in fjøset and whose only job was to keep down the rat and mice population. A quick cuddle with the soft furry cat was worth at least an hour of muck cleaning. But oftentimes Snuppen was too busy hunting, even though Freya tried to bribe her with bits of cheese. Snuppen had a funny little face with lopsided markings, a blob of black over one eye and a white patch over one ear. She had a scratchy little voice you could hardly hear, but she was an excellent hunter.

While Freya sat on the bus, she planned what she would do that afternoon. First, run down and call Lorelei. After a chat, Freya would find bits and bobs in her craft box and make a nice card for Lisbet; something to cheer her up. Then she would ask Mamma if she could make some cookies for Lisbet, with the letter 'L' iced on every one. That way when Lisbet got home from seeing the doctor, she would have something nice to read and eat. As Freya later walked down to the shore to talk to Lorelei, she decided red icing would look best for the 'L' on the cookies.

When she walked in through the kitchen door Freya heard laughter and saw her mother and Tante Nina hugging each other, all smiles.

"I'm so happy for you, Nina!" said Mamma, tucking a stray strand of hair behind her sister-in-law's ear. "You've waited so long."

Tante Nina blushed, her hand resting on her belly. She turned to look at Freya. Her eyes were shining with happiness, her skin radiant, her cheeks rose red. Freya squealed with delight and ran to her aunt putting her arms around her.

"What is it? What is the good news? You look so happy Tante Nina!"

Her aunt squeezed her tight.

"My prayers been answered, at last, Freya!" She crouched down to look into Freya's face. "I'm going to have a baby. Isn't that wonderful?" She looked up at her sister-in-law. "Is it not the most wonderful news you've ever heard?"

Freya felt a fizzing sensation inside her tummy.

"A cousin! A little cousin, to hold and take for walks in the pram and dress up in cute little clothes!" Freya cried.

Tante Nina giggled.

"Yes of course. There will be lots of that. I'm sure you will be a very loving cousin to this baby."

"So, what does Felix say?" Asked Mamma.

"I haven't told him yet. I only just received the phone call half an hour ago with the test results. I thought I would wait until they'd finished the afternoon milking," said Tante Nina.

Mamma nodded.

"Well, perhaps it's time we baked something delicious for this occasion."

"Yes! Yes, let's do that!" Freya cried joyfully.

"What's all the noise?" said Lisbet from the foot of the stairs. "It's like a train station in here." She walked through to the lounge room, a sullen expression on her face. For a second, Tante Nina's smile slipped.

"How is she?" Tante Nina asked Mamma.

Mamma shook her head.

"No change. But the counsellor says it's early days."

"Counsellor?" said Freya, looking from one woman to the other. "What's a counsellor?"

"It's a special kind of doctor who helps people with emotional problems, Freya," said Tante Nina. "The idea is to help them sort through what's happened to them and figure out how to be happy again, I suppose." She sighed. "If only we could help Lisbet," she said sadly.

"Well I thought if I made her a card and some cookies with a capital L on them it would brighten her up a bit," said Freya. "But now I'm not so sure," she said, staring at the door through which her sister had just disappeared.

"Why don't you go in and tell her the good news?" Mamma suggested to Tante Nina.

"Of course."

Just as Freya went to follow, Mamma said, "Freya, you can help me here. Leave your sister and Tante Nina some privacy."

"Why does Lisbet need privacy?" said Freya.

"She just does," replied Mamma firmly.

"But what's wrong with her?" demanded Freya. "No one tells me anything!"

"That's because we can't, vennen min," said Mamma. "It's between the counsellor and Lisbet. When she is ready to tell us, she will."

Freya shook her head.

"I don't understand any of this. What could be so bad, that Lisbet can't even tell you, Mamma?"

"I suppose we will find out, won't we?"

Just then Tante Nina emerged from the lounge room, her face rather pale.

"What's wrong?" Said Mamma, worriedly, putting down the metal cooking bowl she had just picked up. "Did she…did she say anything horrible to you?"

"No," said Tante Nina softly. "It's not what she said; it's how she reacted when I told the news." Tante

Nina stared at her sister-in-law. "She was absolutely terrified."

CHAPTER FIFTEEN

At five thirty the three Askvold brothers tramped into the kitchen, their faces reddened by the wind, their deep voices loud in the white painted, wood panelled room, the smell of cows and milking clinging to them.

"I told you," Onkel Stefan laughed. "I was the one who really saved the day!"

Pappa gave him a gentle shove.

"You're dreaming, baby brother." He glanced at Felix, the eldest of the three, who had sat on himself down on the wooden bench against the wall to pull his trouser legs out from inside his socks. "Isn't he, Felix?" Pappa chuckled.

"If he needs attention that badly, give it to him," said Onkel Felix, frowning. "We all know what happened that day."

"Well I guess it depends on whose version of that

day you believe," said Onkel Stefan with a grin, looking like an impish young boy. He winked at Freya. "I'll tell you my version tonight, Freya. I was even younger than you that day and…"

"Nina here?" Asked Onkel Felix suddenly.

Mamma nodded in the direction of the lounge room.

"She's in there, looking through photo albums."

"What for? We've seen them all before," grumbled Onkel Felix getting to his feet. He limped across the room, everyone's eyes watching him. The laughter and happiness had leeched away, like smoke disappearing under the kitchen door. Onkel Stefan went to follow him, a determined look on his face, his hands clenched by his sides. Pappa shook his head and held out his hand to stop his brother.

"Stefan, there's no point. Leave them be."

"Why does he have to be so goddam miserable all the time?" Onkel Stefan said vehemently. Freya stared at her normally jovial uncle. What had happened during the milking? The brothers were used to working together. In fact, to Freya, there was something comforting about the absolute regularity of the milking; twice a day, in any kind of weather. No matter what happened in the lives of the family the milking still had to be done, the cows fed, watered and cared for, electric fences moved in the warmer months to allow them new pastures. Freya had always assumed that her father and uncle enjoyed their work. On occasion she'd walked to the barn and heard her uncle whistling. And her father often sang as he mucked out stalls or drove the tractor with large bales of hay on the back. It was manly work, very physical, not that Mamma wasn't strong or that she didn't lift heavy things. The work that men did was different somehow. The cows were such large and sometimes scary beasts to a small child and it seemed that only Pappa and her uncle had the physical strength and presence to handle them. There was comfort in knowing that your father was strong and capable, always there for you. The night Onkel Stefan arrived he'd swung Freya up in his arms and spun her around the room as if she weighed nothing, which brought a thrill of exhilaration in her throat, as if she were flying through the air like a bird.

But now, that joy had vanished and in its place settled a cold kind of grief, a loss, an empty space inside her heart. She loved Onkel Felix. He had gruff ways of being kind, almost as if he were embarrassed to admit that he cared. One of her treasured possessions was a small, wooden bird he'd carved for her. Onkel Felix was like the brown bears that used to live on Eikeberg island – with the cuddly pelt of fur which made you want to touch them but fascinating and scary in their fierceness and strength.

From the other room came the sounds of murmured conversation. In the kitchen, Pappa and Onkel Stefan had begun discussing calving season, sitting at the table with cups of steaming coffee. In the reprieve before dinner preparation Mamma sat with them, reading her book. The tones in the lounge became harsher and knowing Tante Nina's exciting and joyful news, Freya began to feel angry at her uncle. Without thinking, she stormed into the lounge, hands on hips and glared at him.

"Why can't you ever be happy, Onkel Felix?" Freya pointed at her aunt. "Tante Nina was happy a few moments ago until you ruined it!"

"Freya..." Tante Nina began, a look of consternation on her face.

Onkel Felix frowned at Freya but said nothing. Was he actually listening to her? Freya decided to keep going.

"I'll bet you don't even know what it is! You couldn't even guess. This is the happiest day of her life. What is more important than a beautiful new b..." Freya stopped herself just in time.

Tante Nina smiled and took her husband's hand in hers. Her eyes misted with tears and her bottom lip trembled. "Felix..."

He stared at her. All anger dropped from his face and for a moment his features were handsome, open and caring.

"What is it Nina?"

She sobbed with joy as the words tumbled out. "I'm pregnant, Felix! I'm pregnant! The doctor confirmed it today."

He stared at her. Two emotions passed over his face – the first surprise, then joy. Freya hadn't seen her uncle smile in a very long time.

"Nina..." He shook his head. "How?" His voice cracked with emotion.

She giggled.

"I think you know how."

Even Freya giggled at that.

"But, I thought we couldn't..." He searched his wife's face for the reason.

"So did I," she replied joyfully. He sighed, then held out his arms and she nestled into them. He stroked her hair tenderly. Freya smiled to herself, turned on her heel and went back into the kitchen. Mission accomplished. Mamma's raised eyebrows asked the question. Freya nodded enthusiastically.

"She's told him, Mamma! She told him and he's happy!"

"Told him what?" Said Pappa and Onkel Stefan simultaneously.

Freya looked at her mother for permission. Mamma nodded.

"Tante Nina's pregnant!"

Onkel Stefan whooped for joy. Pappa laughed and slapped his brother on the back.

"Fantastic news!" said Pappa. "We must go in and congratulate them."

Everyone trooped into the lounge room where Tante Nina and Onkel Felix reclined together in each other's arms on the sofa, looking young and in love. The lines of pain had disappeared from Onkel Felix's face and Tante Nina blushed with happiness. Pappa and Onkel Stefan shook their brother's hand and congratulated him, gave their sister-in-law a peck on the cheek. Freya ran to the stairs and called up to the attic rooms.

"Lisbet! You should come down here! Everyone is so happy about the baby." There was no reply. When she returned to the lounge room the adults were all sitting comfortably, chatting about the coming addition to the family.

"Have you thought of any names?" asked Onkel Stefan, grinning. "If it's a boy, I recommend naming him Stefan."

Tante Nina grinned back at him. "That's a nice

idea, but I think perhaps one Stefan Askvold is probably enough."

"Definitely," agreed Pappa. He waved his finger at Onkel Stefan. "Don't you go teaching him your naughty ways, little brother."

"I'll do my best," he replied.

Mamma leaned forward eagerly.

"Nina, what girl's names have you thought of? I'm itching to start knitting baby clothes!"

"Well, I like Sofia and Astrid so far. But I think perhaps we will need to see her face before we truly know which name suits her." Tante Nina turned to smile at her husband lovingly. "And Felix might have some ideas of his own for his daughter. Or son."

Onkel Felix stared down at his wife with an expression of such deep happiness. It was a shock to Freya to see it.

"I'm sure anything you come up with will be perfect, *min kjæreste*, (my darling)," he said.

Freya couldn't help it. She squealed and jumped up and down, clapping her hands. The happiness in the room was like bright orange, pink and yellow light had surrounded them all.

"Well I'm going to come up with the list of my own," she announced. "You never know, I might find the perfect name for my cousin! In fact, I'm going to start right now." She ran from the room to the stairs, clomping up the wooden staircase, not caring if she disturbed her sister, ran straight to her room, got out her notebook and pen and settled herself on her bed. What fantastic news she would have to tell Lorelei tomorrow!

CHAPTER SIXTEEN

For dinner that night they had Tante Nina's favourite – sausages and potato mash with peas and brown sauce. And for dessert, *karamellpudding*. Even Lisbet came down, pale faced and silent to eat with them, but wouldn't engage in any conversation. Tante Nina's words came back to Freya – 'she was absolutely terrified.' Freya couldn't think of a single reason why Lisbet would be so afraid of Tante Nina's pregnancy. It didn't make any sense. Throughout dinner she glanced at Lisbet's face constantly, looking for clues.

After dinner they played board games, which they hadn't done since Christmas. Even Onkel Felix joined in. He seemed a different person, or perhaps the person he had hidden inside for many years. He was even civil towards Mamma. Apart from Lisbet's silence, it seemed to Freya that her family felt whole again. Onkel Stefan's booming laugh and cheeky smile seemed to ignite the conversation with energy, the pulse rippling out to everyone. She stared at her uncle with adoration. He was the best thing that had happened in their lives for a very long time and she hoped that he had decided to move back to Eikeberg island for good.

The next day was Saturday. After breakfast Mamma announced that she was taking a basket of goodies over to Tante Nina. The basket included a soft pale yellow knitted blanket Mamma had made when Freya was born. Freya dug her fingers into the downy soft wool and leaned in to smell the clean fragrance. She smiled up at her mother.

"I wish I could remember being a baby. I can just imagine sleeping in my little wooden crib that Pappa made, snuggling under this blanket!"

Mamma stroked her hair.

"Lille venn, you were such a good baby. Slept most of the night, no feeding problems. Smiled such a lot! You were my joy. And Pappa's little angel."

"Pappa's little angel," sneered Lisbet from the doorway. Freya turned her head away from her sister. She just did not want to deal with Lisbet's anger right now. Why did she have to spoil everything?

"Lisbet, kjære venn, you didn't come down for breakfast." Mamma moved over to her elder daughter and stroked her arm. "You look pale, Liebling. You must eat. How about I make you a cup of tea and some eggs on toast?"

Lisbet screwed up her face.

"No thank you. I feel sick." Her eyes looked red, as if she'd been crying and Freya felt mean for the thoughts she'd had about her sister. A crushing sense of sorrow squeezed Freya's heart. Before she could think about it, she blurted out her thoughts.

"Lisbet, what's wrong? I feel like you're so sad."

Lisbet's eyes filled instantly with tears, her face flushed bright red.

"Shut up Freya! Just shut up and leave me alone! It's none of your business." She turned and ran up the stairs. Freya burst into tears and clung to Mamma's skirt.

"I know, lille venn, you want to help and that is normal. You love your sister, don't you?" She rubbed small circles in the middle of Freya's back. Warmth spread from her mother's hand and Freya quietened down. "When we get back from visiting Tante Nina, Pappa and I are taking Lisbet to her appointment."

"On a Saturday?" Freya said, sniffing.

"Yes. Things are…getting a bit too difficult to deal with."

"Does the doctor know what it is yet?"

"The counsellor. Yes, I think she has an idea, but right now we're just hoping Lisbet will trust her enough to tell her the truth."

"Why wouldn't she? Why wouldn't Lisbet tell the counsellor what's wrong?"

Mamma crouched down and put the basket on the floor beside her. Looking into Freya's eyes tenderly she said,

"Sometimes the things that are deep in our heart, that hurt us the most, are the hardest to share. I hope, my little Freya, that you never have to experience this."

Freya put her arms around her mother's neck.

"Me too. I hope I never feel like Lisbet does."

CHAPTER SEVENTEEN

That afternoon, Tante Nina came over to look after Freya while Mamma and Pappa took Lisbet to Elveby to see the counsellor.

"Hello, my darling little Freya!" Exclaimed Tante Nina as she came through the back door, her face pink and shiny with happiness. Freya looked up from where she had been drawing at the kitchen table. She noticed that her aunt wore a new top, long and flared out below the waist. "You like my swing top?" Tante Nina asked. "It's for when the baby starts to get big." She patted her stomach.

"It's nice. Tante Nina, would you like to see my drawing?" Freya said, holding out the colourful picture.

Her aunt took it.

"It's beautiful Freya," she said softly. "I love the way you've drawn Onkel Felix looking happy, holding the baby. And the pram - very nice too." Her eyes twinkled at Freya.

"He smiled a lot yesterday," Freya said. "I really like it when Onkel Felix smiles like that."

"So do I," her aunt answered softly. "So do I. Now, shall we make some marzipan ducks?"

"Really? And it's not even Christmas!"

"No," Tante Nina said, bending down to get out the mixing bowl from the cupboard. "But it's a special time, isn't it? And why not celebrate with something that we all love? Now, put on your apron and let's begin."

An hour later a tray of marzipan ducks in varying sizes and shapes sat on a tray in the middle of the kitchen table. They were decorated with tiny edible silver beads for eyes and swam in little green coloured marzipan puddles because it was too difficult to make feet strong enough for them to stand up. Freya had of course licked the mixing bowl and sneaked a few pieces of marzipan when Tante Nina wasn't looking. She couldn't wait until her parents got home to show them her amazing little creations. And of course eat a few.

It was mid-afternoon when Onkel Stefan came through the door looking very pleased with himself.

"Where have you been Onkel Stefan?" Asked Freya, licking the last of the marzipan from her fingers and wiping her hands on her apron.

"I've been to town. Elveby certainly has grown in the last few years that I've been away. I can't believe how many houses have sprung up. Ooh, is that marzipan?" He went to pick up one of the ducks. Freya leapt in front of him.

"Ah-ah!" She wagged a finger. "You can't touch

them until after dinner, Onkel Stefan!"

He grinned, and went to the kettle to make himself a cup of tea.

"So, Nina, I must say you look absolutely radiant. More beautiful than ever."

She smiled shyly, her hands in the sudsy sink. He picked up a tea towel and started drying the dishes that were in the rack.

"You know, it could have been different, this baby and…things," he said thoughtfully.

Tante Nina flicked a glance towards Freya nervously. She lowered her voice to answer.

"Let's not talk about this now, Stefan. It's not the time or the place. And in any case, that's water under the bridge, isn't it?" She looked up into his face with her beautiful blue eyes. Onkel Stefan shrugged. Freya thought that if she concentrated very hard she would understand the secret message passing between the two adults. But it seemed very unclear to her what they were talking about.

They moved to the lounge room, where Tante Nina again picked up the photo albums. Onkel Stefan sat on one side of her, Freya the other as they leafed through an old, battered album with lots of black-and-white photographs of three boys and their growing years.

Freya pointed to a photo of Onkel Stefan as a baby and laughed out loud.

"You look so funny! I didn't realise you had such curly blonde hair."

He chuckled.

"And boy, did I get teased about it!"

"Do you remember yesterday you were going to

tell me about that story from when the three of you were boys?"

Onkel Stefan leaned back and smiled.

"Well, we used to swim at a special little spot, further west of here."

"Still on the island?" Freya asked.

"Yes. The sea dumps very finely crushed up rock there, which is almost like sand. We used to call it our beach and it was a favourite spot to go swimming. The only problem with that spot is that the tides can form a rip. Not very often, but it can be quite dangerous. So we always brought with us an old surfboard that Felix got from somewhere. Just in case. Anyway, one day it was a really beautiful, hot, sunny day and we'd been swimming for quite a while. So we came onto the beach to lie on our towels and eat our sandwiches. And then some tourists came along. Two families actually – four adults and five children. You should have seen your uncle Felix's face! He always thought it was *our* private beach that no one else should know about. So when these tourists turned up his face looked like a thundercloud. Anyway, we were joking around, throwing sand at each other, trying to build sand castles but having very little success because the sand was too dry. The tourists had gone into the water, all of them, including the children. They were having a great time, splashing, the kids shrieking with joy and fun. And then, suddenly, Felix looked up at them and said really quietly, "Something's wrong." I didn't realise he was serious at first. Your Pappa was the first one into the water. He was like a streak of lightning! Straight in, swimming very swiftly and strongly towards the families. The children were spluttering and crying and the adults were trying to keep them calm but the riptide was pulling them out into the middle of the fjord."

"Oh no! Would they have drowned?" Freya asked, feeling a cold sensation in her stomach.

Onkel Stefan nodded.

"Almost certainly. They were already tired and the children were quite young, the youngest was probably three and the eldest was about eight."

"How old were you at the time, Onkel Stefan?"

"I was twelve, your Pappa was fourteen and Onkel Felix was sixteen. Anyway, your Pappa started bringing back two of the small children and Onkel Felix was on the shore helping him bring them in to the sand. And that seemed to go well, but the tide was taking the rest of them so fast. Even I could tell by the sounds of the adults' voices that they were very scared. So I grabbed the surfboard and I rushed into the water with it, past Onkel Felix and past your Pappa, straight out to the people. I instructed them to hang onto the board so that I could paddle it back into shore, but they were so frightened they didn't listen to me. After all, I was only a young boy. Then Onkel Felix swam out and somehow we managed to get two of the adults and one of the small children onto the board. I swam right at the back and kicked my legs as hard as I could to push it towards shore. Onkel Felix stayed with the last adult and child, treading water. I tell you what, it was darn hard work getting back to shore. That rip was extremely strong."

"You must've been so scared! Did you really think you were going to make it?" said Freya.

"Such a brave thing for such a young boy to do!" exclaimed Tante Nina, her eyes wide.

"Well, there wasn't much time to think about it really. We all just clicked into action and did what we could to rescue them. We did three trips in the end. And everyone was saved. And I," Onkel Stefan patted his chest proudly. "Was interviewed for the local newspaper. We might have a copy of it around here somewhere. Local pint-sized hero and all that."

"Wow, Onkel Stefan, I had no idea! Pappa and Onkel Felix have never told the whole story," said Freya.

"Well," a lazy smile spread over Onkel Stefan's handsome face. "Probably because I was the hero and I was the youngest. And they didn't want to share the glory."

Tante Nina giggled and poked Onkel Stefan in the ribs.

"Still cheeky as ever, aren't you?" She said with affection.

"Well isn't this cosy?" said an angry voice from the doorway. Freya spun to see Onkel Felix standing there, frowning at them all.

"Felix," Tante Nina began. "We were just…"

"I can see what you are doing! You two. Always sniggering behind my back. Always colluding. Wouldn't surprise me if that's not all you're doing."

"Felix, come on, that's a bit harsh." Onkel Stefan said, rising from the sofa.

"Shut up Stefan!" Onkel Felix's face was red with anger. Freya could feel it in waves of hate and it frightened her. She whimpered and Tante Nina pulled her close.

"Felix, you're frightening Freya."

"You!" He said to his wife, his dark brows drawn

down in a sharp V. He spoke to her as if she were some kind of stray dog that had come to the back door, begging for food. "For years and years and years – nothing. No baby. And suddenly he turns up," Onkel Felix pointed a shaking finger at his youngest brother. "And bingo! You're pregnant. How miraculous."

"Now that's enough!" Onkel Stefan raised his voice in indignation. "How dare you speak to Nina like that! You've got no grounds to accuse her of anything! Apologise immediately."

Onkel Felix slouched on one hip.

"Or what? You're going to teach me a lesson, are you, little brother?"

"Felix." Onkel Stefan sighed. "We're not children. We're supposed to be setting a good example for Freya here. Can't we discuss this reasonably, like adults?"

"Yes, Felix, please! Not in front of Freya. This is a private matter between us. Please don't drag an innocent girl into this hateful scene. These are hurts that have been let fester for far too long," Tante Nine implored.

"Oh, so you admit there are hurts, do you? You admit you have hurt me?"

Tante Nina got to her feet.

"Felix, I'm not going to discuss this with you now. Not in front of Freya. Let's go home and we'll talk about it there." She went to walk past him and his arm flashed out to stop her. Onkel Stefan made a noise deep in his throat. Suddenly the room was awful, out-of-control, with the people she loved most acting like they were enemies. Freya couldn't bear it and burst into tears.

"See what you've done Felix?" Tante Nina cried, pulling Freya close again. His hands clenched beside him but he said nothing, turned awkwardly on his good leg and walked out of the room. Onkel Stefan bent and picked Freya up and held her close in his arms, where she buried her head on his shoulder and cried.

"There, there, Freya. My sweet little niece. Such old hurts and such innocent young ears to hear them."

"But why?" Freya wailed.

"I don't know," said Onkel Stefan truthfully. "But hey," he tickled under her chin. "How about we sneak into the kitchen and grab some marzipan?" He put her down. "We can take it outside. I know where there is a bird's nest. And when I was walking past it earlier today I heard some mysterious little noises from inside it."

Freya looked up at her uncle's face.

"Really? Little noises? Like tiny baby birds squeaking?"

He nodded. Taking her hand they walked into the empty kitchen. Onkel Stefan chose the biggest, fattest marzipan duck. Freya chose the second-biggest, and grinning at each other, they went outside.

CHAPTER EIGHTEEN

Lisbet came through the door pale faced and silent later that day, her parents following, equally silent. Freya sat at the kitchen table drawing with Tante Nina and watched as they walked by. Pappa went straight into the lounge room and moments later the television came to life. Mamma stood for a moment in the middle of the kitchen, a little dazed, then seemed to remember where she was and brightened suddenly.

"Freya, I hope you were well behaved for Tante Nina?" She stroked Freya's hair.

"Yes, of course!" Freya reassured her. She pointed to a tray on the bench. "We even made marzipan ducks!"

"How wonderful!" Mamma said, looking them over appreciatively. "May I try one?"

"Well, it's nearly dinner time... But I think I will

let you have one. Just one," Freya said, wagging a finger with mock seriousness.

Tante Nina giggled.

"She has been absolutely perfect. No trouble at all. We always have fun together, don't we lille venn?"

"Uh huh. And we were looking at photos of Pappa when he was a boy." Freya added. Her mood suddenly fell. "And then Onkel Felix came in and got angry."

Mamma and Tante Nina exchanged looks of concern, but said nothing.

"And then Onkel Stefan took me outside and showed me a bird's nest and I heard the little birds squeaking inside it!"

"That's amazing!" said Mamma with a smile. "We will have to keep an eye on that nest and hopefully see the fledglings when they are ready to fly for the first time. Wouldn't that be wonderful?"

"Oh, yes! I've never seen a baby bird leave the nest. Do you think Pappa would let you borrow his camera?"

"I'm sure he would," Mamma said, sitting down beside Freya.

Tante Nina got up.

"Well I'd better be getting back. The afternoon milking has finished."

"Stefan helped Felix then?" Mamma asked.

Tante Nina shrugged.

"I guess so. Today I am past the point of caring."

"Nina! I've never heard you speak like this," Mamma said getting to her feet. Tante Nina's face became red and tears fell from her eyes. Mamma took her into a long embrace. "My dear Nina, what you have been through! It's just not fair."

Tante Nina sniffed and pulled away gently. She looked into the face of her sister-in-law.

"You have your share of worries, Gretchen," she said solemnly. "Don't worry about me. I'll be fine." She placed a protective hand on her tummy. "And now Felix has someone else to think about, hopefully things will change."

"I hope you're right," said Mamma.

A tray of dinner was taken up to Lisbet that evening. As Freya left it on the floor outside her sister's door she wondered what the counsellor had said. And whether her sister had at last confided the truth. Again Freya wondered what could be so bad that Lisbet could not tell her own parents. In Freya's world the worst she could think of was that Lisbet had broken or stolen something.

That evening Mamma brought down her knitting basket of wool and needles and began looking through the patterns of baby clothes. As she sat in her favourite armchair, under the golden glow of the floor lamp, Mamma looked happy and contented. Pappa sat reading the newspaper.

"Mamma, do you think you could teach me to knit?" Freya asked as she leafed through pattern booklets. There were so many cute and cuddly bonnets and jackets and booties and mittens. Mamma took a ball of softest pale yellow wool and began casting stitches onto the wooden knitting needle.

"Well, I suppose, but do you remember the last time I tried to teach you, Freya? You just got so angry and frustrated. It was no fun for me at all. I will only teach you if you are ready to persist and not throw it away when you drop a stitch or it's too tight."

"I'm ready!" Freya said eagerly. "And I even know which colour I want to use. That pale lavender colour looks nice. I could make some booties, or a jacket..."

"Freya, I think you should start with something simple," cautioned Mamma. "Perhaps a scarf?"

"A scarf? But that's boring! I want to make something cute!"

Mamma sighed.

"This is why I haven't taught you to knit yet, Freya. You are too impatient. Knitting requires a lot of patience. You've seen me pull up stitches many times before I am happy with it. This is what knitting is like. Even when you follow a pattern you'll make mistakes."

"I understand, I really do," Freya insisted. "I just want to make something pretty for Tante Nina because she was so sad today."

"Freya," Pappa said kindly but firmly. "It is not your responsibility to make us adults happy. Sometimes there are things even we cannot fix."

"But I love Tante Nina and she deserves to be happy!" Freya said stubbornly. "And sometimes Onkel Felix is so mean to her!"

Pappa put down the paper and folded it carefully.

"There are things you don't know, Freya and are too young to understand. Things that happened before you were born."

"What things?"

"Private things," he said gravely. "Things that only adults can talk about. Things only adults understand."

"But he's not just mean to Tante Nina, he's mean to Mamma too. And I hate that!" Freya said hotly.

"I understand that Freya," Pappa said patiently.

"But you never say anything! You don't defend Mamma when he says mean things to her!" Freya cried passionately.

"Freya," Mamma said gently, flicking a worried glance at her husband. "I think it might be time for you to get ready for bed."

"But why? Why aren't I allowed to be angry at Onkel Felix?"

Pappa looked at Mamma, his brows raised.

Mamma sighed.

"She has a point, Torstein." She shrugged and went on knitting.

Pappa sighed too, staring down at his fingernails.

"I... I feel sorry about that, Freya. I do. It's just..." He raised his head and looked straight into his daughter's eyes. "I cannot control my brother's behaviour. He's a grown man."

"Then he should stay away!"

Pappa made an exasperated sound.

"It's not that simple. We run the dairy together. He's my brother. I cannot tell him what to do. It's complicated."

Freya stared at her father, seeing someone new, someone who wasn't just tall and strong and always right. She saw a man who had doubts about himself. Inside him was that little boy in the photo albums, the second son. And she knew what it was like to be the second born. Freya chewed her lip. She loved her big sister. But she was struggling to get used to this new, sullen version; this dreadfully unhappy, angry girl who lashed out at everyone. Just like Onkel Felix.

Someone, Freya decided, *someone outside the family* must have hurt Lisbet.

"Freya, time for bed." Pappa said. "Now, please."

Freya kissed them both goodnight and climbed the stairs feeling frustrated. She had been unable to call Lorelei that day, to tell her about it, despite sitting on the rock and singing for half an hour. In her heart Freya felt an uneasy restless motion, like small, unsettled waves crinkling to the shore. And the coldness of her doubts began to grow.

CHAPTER NINETEEN

Freya woke next morning to the sound of voices downstairs. Raised voices. She crept barefoot out of her room, careful to avoid the squeaky floorboards. Lisbet's closed door was a clear message she didn't want to be disturbed. At the top of the staircase Freya stood, wide-eyed and listened. Tante Nina's voice had tears in it. Mamma's voice was deep and soothing. And Pappa's bass voice had a hard edge; urgent, almost demanding. Freya crept closer.

The fourth step protested loudly with a sharp CRACK! Freya froze, her hand on the rail, biting her lip in concentration. The voices downstairs hushed, then began again in whispered earnest. As she reached the tenth step, Freya paused and sat down slowly. She knew her feet would be visible to those downstairs through the balustrades, but hoped if she sat absolutely still they wouldn't know she was there. Her patience was rewarded.

"What are you going to do, Nina?" Asked Mamma gently.

"I don't know!" Wailed Tante Nina. "He's just so angry. I've never seen him like this before!"

Freya heard her father's deep sigh.

"He's never *been* like this before. Didn't speak a single word to me during milking this morning. Not one word. I don't understand him. It should be a joyous time for the two of you, but instead he's raking over old hurts, old miseries. It doesn't make any sense."

"It does if you're Felix," answered Tante Nina firmly. "He's never forgiven you, Gretchen. I've tried so hard over the years to get him to let go of it, but he refuses. He blames you and I fear he always will. It's like a pot simmering on the stove until there is nothing left but a hard, black mess."

Freya heard her mother's voice murmur, but the words were indistinct.

"Well, I'm not about to let this keep happening. It's hurting everyone in the family." Pappa sounded resolute. Freya had heard this tone before and she knew her father would be immovable once he had made this sort of decision. "I'll find him and sort this out, once and for all," said Pappa. The back door opened.

"Torstein," Mamma begged. "Don't be too hard on your brother. It was, after all, my fault. We cannot change the past. And every day I see the pain it causes him."

"Gretchen, you are my wife. And I will not allow my brother to destroy our family's happiness because of something that happened so long ago. Whoever was at fault at the time."

"But it was an accident, wasn't it?" Tante Nina's voice had a hint of hysteria in it. "Before I met him. You would never hurt my Felix, Gretchen. I know you."

"It was…unfortunate," Mamma replied. "I should not have been driving the tractor in the first place. But the boys needed my help. And I foolishly thought I knew what I was doing. After all, I had grown up in a farming district in Germany."

"Min kjæreste Gretchen," Pappa said gently. "Once and for all, it was *not your fault*. We knew the risk when we asked you to help. We knew you didn't know how to drive a tractor properly. We knew a two minute lesson was inadequate, but we couldn't move that lumber without a third person. Accidents happen." Pappa's voice grew angry. "And Felix needs to grow up and get over this! Or he will lose everything he has - his wife, his new baby, everything that matters."

Sitting on the tenth step, Freya's breath felt like cottonwool in her lungs. What was this story she'd never heard before? Pieces of the family puzzle were beginning to slot into place in her mind. Onkel Felix had always been mean to Mamma.

And now she understood why.

She wanted to race down the stairs and ask to hear the full story, to understand what happened that day. But Freya knew, deep in her bones, that this story belonged to the adults, to a different time. Even the adults were struggling to deal with it. She resolved to talk to Lorelei about it today. Freya tiptoed back up the stairs to her room and got dressed. She pulled out her notebook, sat on her bed and wrote a few lines.

Today I heard a story about my Mamma. She did something a long time ago that hurt Onkel Felix. And this is why he has a limp and is in pain all the time. Why didn't anyone tell me? I should have known! And then I wouldn't feel so angry at him. It was an accident, so why is he so mean about it? Mamma would never hurt anyone. I love her so much! She is the best mamma in the world. Sometimes I think my heart isn't big enough to hold all the love. And Pappa too of course! And even Lisbet though she is mean to me. She has a hurt too, but I don't think it's her hip. She's not limping. I think the hurt is inside her mind. And you can't put a bandage on that.

Down by the shoreline Freya sat on her usual rounded rock, warmed by the morning sun. Grey, lumpy clouds had gathered overhead and the breeze had picked up. She untied the jacket from around her waist and put it on, pulling the hood over her head. Then she began to sing, her eyes scanning the grey fjord. Tiny white waves pushed each other aside as they aimed for the shore. Pappa had said the best time to fish was in weather such as this, when humans would rather be indoors. She pictured her father and Onkel Felix out in their boat, fishing lines in hand, laughing and having fun. It seemed like a dream, that image. From someone else's life. As she sang the second verse for the second time Freya began to worry that Lorelei had abandoned her. She'd become so used to having Lorelei to confide in, someone who didn't ask embarrassing or pointless questions. Someone who just listened and occasionally made a squawking noise and pointed at the water. Someone who didn't tell her she was being silly or that children "…

didn't need to know such things."

Then she heard a splash to her left and with joy in her heart Freya stood, watching the water intently. Lorelei emerged like a seal – smooth and effortless. She sat on her own rock and turned to look at Freya, with absolutely no expression on her face. Freya watched Lorelei's double blinking eyes, so inhuman yet so pretty. Lorelei's small mouth opened and she made a tiny chittering sound while gesturing to Freya, her small, white, pointed teeth gleaming.

"What is it?" Freya asked. "What is it you want me to do?"

There was an urgency to Lorelei's voice as she made the chittering sound again and pointed out to the fjord.

Freya looked out across the great expanse of water, across to the other side where the small town of Stranda sat sheltered at the base of the mountains. She shrugged and held up her palms to Lorelei.

"I don't understand. I'm sorry. I didn't even bring you anything to eat today. I'm too worried about my family. Tante Nina is so upset because Onkel Felix is angry. And he's angry at Mamma which doesn't help at all. Mamma couldn't help it! It was an accident! Why can't the adults get over these things?" Freya hung her head, studying her finger nails. Then her gaze shifted to the small, speckled rocks at her feet, the water gliding over them, white foam and tiny bits of seaweed floating on its surface.

Lorelei squawked urgently. Freya's head snapped up.

"What? What is it?"

Lorelei slapped her chest with both hands forcefully. She made the chittering sound again and pointed out to the water. She held out her arms to Freya, her thin lips trembling. Freya felt tears come to her eyes. She could feel Lorelei's distress but she didn't know what to do. Getting to her feet she moved slowly towards the havfrue, closer than she'd ever been before. She could smell the wildness of Lorelei, the deep fathoms of the sea and an ancient knowledge. But she did not smell danger, just an urgency she didn't quite understand.

Up close, Lorelei's skin was smooth and flawless, tinged green and grey. Her arms were thin and muscular. Her eyes were larger than a human's and far apart, their goat-like pupils mesmerising.

Suddenly Lorelei reached out and grabbed Freya's hand. Her ice cold touch was shocking. Freya had imagined her to be warm blooded. Lorelei's long fingers wrapped around Freya's wrist and tugged her close. Freya felt a tingle of excitement and fear, but she didn't pull back against the havfrue's grip. Instead she dropped to her haunches beside her. Freya reached out very slowly, wanting to touch the scales on Lorelei's lower body. Lorelei doubled blinked down at her but made no move to refuse.

Lorelei's scaled skin was incredibly soft. The havfrue shifted her body ever so slightly and all the scales stood up for a few seconds. Freya giggled and ran her fingers over this surface. She looked up at her friend's face.

"It's wonderful. Your skin... It's so amazing! It feels like wet feathers," she said softly. Lorelei grunted deep in her throat. It was not a sound of annoyance but of acknowledgement. Lorelei let go of Freya's hand and ran a nail-less fingertip down Freya's cheek. Staring at Freya intently she opened her mouth and a rough gurgling sound emerged through her pointed teeth. It was somewhere between a growl and a murmur. Her breath smelled of rotten fish and her body gave off an odour like sunbaked seaweed. Such unpleasant smells to human nostrils, but to Freya it was just natural. Lorelei was a princess of the deep and this was how they smelled.

"I know you don't understand me," Freya said. "And I don't know if you even have a family, but my family is in a bit of a mess at the moment. Lisbet is so unhappy and no one seems to know why. Tante Nina is pregnant, at last, and unhappy, which is just wrong. Onkel Felix is angry over something that no one can fix. Mamma is sad and feels guilty for something she can't change. And Pappa, who is usually so calm and kind and always knows what to do isn't himself." Freya's voice rose with fear. "And Onkel Stefan took the ferry to town yesterday and didn't come back last night. And I hope nothing bad has happened to him!"

Lorelei grunted, double blinked, then her pointy tongue flashed out to moisten her lips. Turning her head, Freya stared up at her family home, Fjellheim, flanked by the big red barn built hundreds of years before. The forest curved behind both buildings like a shield. The white wooden walls of her home were usually such a comfort. Its large downstairs windows looked out over the fjord with confidence. She had always felt safe within its walls. Generations of children had grown up in the house, running up and down the painted wooden stairs, sleeping in the small attic rooms with their low pine ceilings, waking to the sound of birds cheeping in the trees outside and sunlight streaming through the small window.

But as she stared at the white house now, Freya imagined a smoky, dark spirit swooping around the house and barn, trying to get inside through any crack. She imagined it plunging into the darkness of the cellar and secretly listening to all their conversations, it's long, dark face, wide gaping mouth and hollowed, black eyes.

CHAPTER TWENTY

When she returned from seeing Lorelei, the house was quiet and empty downstairs. There were no delicious food smells. The cold stove hulked by the empty sink. Clean tea towels hung neatly on the oven door. No radio or TV sounds came from the lounge room. Freya raced up to her sister's bedroom and banged on the door.

"Lisbet! Lisbet, you have to help me!"

"What do you want, Freya? Why are you bothering me?"

"Don't you know what's happening in this family? Don't you even care?"

There was a strangled cry of rage from inside the room and then the door was flung open. Red faced Lisbet, blonde hair in disarray, stared at her sister angrily.

"What is so important that you have to disturb me? What? What is it?"

Staring at her sister's face Freya was suddenly overcome and burst into tears. Silence followed. Lisbet just stood there. And then her voice was softer.

"Freya, what's wrong?"

"Can I come in please?" Freya asked hopefully.

Lisbet's face relaxed a little.

"Come on then. But don't touch anything."

Freya sat on the rumpled bed.

"Everything is horrible!" She cried, unable to hold it in any longer. Lisbet silently handed Freya a tissue then sat beside her, rigid and upright. Freya was expecting a hug, but this was the new Lisbet; the self-contained, angry, curled up Lisbet who didn't need anyone.

Freya struggled between sobs to get the words out.

"Onkel Felix… is angry at… Mamma because… she hurt him. Tante Nina… is upset because Onkel Felix is… horrible to her. Mamma feels guilty… for something that happened so long ago that she… can't change. And Pappa doesn't even understand his own brother!" Her voice trailed off to an anguished whisper. "What's wrong with this family?"

Lisbet didn't reply, her back straight, her eyes staring straight ahead.

"It feels like there's some creepy monster flying around this house making everybody miserable," Freya added.

Silence.

And then a warm hand rested in the middle of Freya's back and began making slow circles, just like Mamma did. Freya leaned into her sister and snuggled under her arm. For a long moment neither spoke. Freya just listened to her sister's heart beating, and the soothing sound of her breathing. She didn't want this moment to end. She didn't want to break the spell.

Lisbet pulled away gently and looked into Freya's eyes.

"Now what's this about Mamma? What accident?"

"There was a tractor accident. A long time ago. Onkel Felix got hurt."

"But why is that Mamma's fault?"

"Because Mamma was driving the tractor. And she didn't really know what she was doing. And the accident happened. And Onkel Felix has been angry at her ever since."

Lisbet frowned.

"So it was an accident. A long time ago. And he's still blaming Mamma?"

Freya nodded.

"That's what they said. And now he's upsetting Tante Nina too. And she's got this beautiful little baby growing inside her. Will it hurt the baby, Lisbet? Will it hurt the baby to be around so much unhappiness? Will the baby come out depressed? Or angry even?"

Lisbet sucked in a breath. For a moment Freya thought she had said something horrifically wrong. Lisbet's face crumpled. She raised her hands and rubbed at her temples. Then she took a deep breath, stared down at her hands and smiled sadly.

"I think a baby comes out brand-new, and then it starts to learn about the world. But when it's brand-new it doesn't know any of these old hurts and bad memories. It's innocent." Lisbet took Freya's face between her hands. "And if we are really nice to this new cousin, if we are sweet and loving and thoughtful and fun, then I'm sure it will have good memories instead of bad." Lisbet withdrew her hands and swivelled to look out the window.

"Lisbet," Freya said, watching her. "You've been a pretty good big sister to me. Even when you're mean and I don't like you very much I still think you're a good big sister. Because you've got a good heart."

Lisbet bowed her head and glistening tears fell, catching the light. Now it was Freya's turn to rub warm circles on her sister's back, but it felt like rubbing a wall. There was unbreakable resistance there, like a tough shell around Lisbet. Love and compassion could flow through to the people outside her, but would not be accepted within.

"Freya, you must promise me something." Lisbet suddenly turned to her sister. "You must promise me, cross your heart and hope to die."

Freya nodded, holding in her breath.

"Something happened to me. But I can't talk about it. And I really, really need you not to ask me. Can you do that?"

Freya just stared at her sister, disappointed.

"I know you want to know what it is. And I know Mamma and Pappa do too. But I'm just not ready to tell anyone yet."

"Is it that awful?" Freya asked.

Lisbet shook her head.

"I don't want to talk about it. And I really need you to respect this. And let me deal with it my way. Okay?"

Freya said nothing. She felt an emptiness open up between them.

"I know you're disappointed. You think that I don't trust you." Lisbet shook her fair head. "But it's not that at all. If I could tell you, I would. But it's complicated. Perhaps when you're a bit older…"

Freya shot up from the bed angrily.

"Why does everyone keep saying that to me? I'm sick of hearing it! I know things! I'm old enough to understand things! But no one else seems to realise that."

Lisbet hung her head and for a moment Freya thought she had made a sister cry again. She rushed to her side and touched Lisbet's white-gold hair.

"I'm sorry, Lisbet. I'm sorry! If I really was a bit more grown-up I wouldn't get angry at you, would I? I'd just accept what you said. And give you the privacy."

Lisbet looked up.

"Thank you. Thanks for understanding, little sister." She hugged Freya tight and murmured in her hair. "You're the best sister I could ever have."

Freya could feel Lisbet holding back sobs but she didn't want to make it worse. She got up and went to the door. With her fingers on the handle she turned. Lisbet sat in a halo of light, as if she had found a moment of peace, a moment to hold onto.

"I'm going to leave you alone now," Freya said. "And I'm not going to ask you what's wrong again. I promise."

"Thanks."

"Do you think you'll be coming to school tomorrow?"

"I don't know. See how I feel."

"Okay. See you at lunch maybe?"

Lisbet smiled bravely.

"Sure."

CHAPTER TWENTY ONE

For something special for Sunday lunch, Mamma announced they would have a picnic outside on the veranda. Freya's job was to lay the outdoor table with a cloth, pretty plates and their best cutlery. The sun broke through wispy white clouds shining down on Freya, filling her with happiness. She hummed while she worked, placing everything exactly right, wanting it to be perfect for Lisbet.

Mamma had made fried chicken, a delicious salad and fresh bread rolls. As she smothered a thick layer of butter on her crusty roll, Freya smiled at Lisbet and winked. To her surprise Lisbet winked back. Mamma looked from one to the other and smiled.

"Are my two lovely daughters getting along today?"

At these words Lisbet's face clouded over.

"So? Is there anything wrong with that?"

Pappa put down his fork, which clanged onto his plate.

"Lisbet, you will apologise to your mother. She has made a magnificent lunch and I do not appreciate your tone."

Lisbet frowned, a deep furrow between her brows and Freya felt certain that an angry outburst was about to issue from her sister's mouth. But Lisbet sighed and turned to her mother and said quietly,

"Sorry Mamma. Lunch is delicious."

They went on eating happily, watching the seagulls chasing each other down at the shoreline, picking at various bits and pieces washed up onto the rocks. The fjord was smooth and dark green today. The big round mountain on the opposite side of the fjord, called Bollen, had a very faint dusting of snow.

"Pappa, did Bollen get some snow last night? It didn't seem that cold." Freya said.

"A couple of nights ago, actually." He loaded up his fork and shoved it into his mouth, munching noisily, a look of satisfaction on his face. "Gretchen, this fried chicken is the best you've ever made."

Mamma smiled and blushed a little.

"Thank you. I tried some different herbs today."

"Are we really going to pretend that everything is all right?" Said Lisbet quietly, with a dark edge to her voice.

Her father looked at her.

"Why not? There is nothing wrong in this family. We love each other, we live in a beautiful place, we have food on the table and a big house. Of course everything is all right."

"If you say so," Lisbet said, turning back to her food. Freya was itching to say something, itching to say that there was something dreadfully wrong in Lisbet's world, even if everyone else was fine. But she had promised not to meddle, not to ask and she figured that included making comments too. She wanted to prove that she wasn't some silly little girl, but someone who could be relied upon and think before she spoke.

"However," her father said, sitting back in his chair and putting his cutlery down. "I do take your point, Lisbet. There are problems within the extended family. And it is up to us to keep things going, to be good, kind, thoughtful people. Reliable and honest."

"Wouldn't being honest mean telling your brother he's being stupid and selfish?" Lisbet said, defiance in her face.

"Lisbet!" Mamma said in surprise.

"I'm sorry, Mamma, but Onkel Felix is being an idiot. And, of course, I can't say anything because *I'm just a child*. He doesn't seem to care about Tante Nina. He doesn't seem to even care about his unborn child. All he cares about is wrongs from the past." Lisbet daintily placed a forkful of food into her mouth. A seagull landed on the railing next to Pappa, ogling his plate with a cheeky, bright orange eye. Pappa shooed it away irritably.

"I appreciate you defending me," said Mamma softly, wiping her mouth with a napkin. "But we cannot be forcing people to change, we cannot be forcing them to accept things, we certainly cannot make them forgive."

"So what do you do, in a family, when one of the

family members is being cruel and making everyone else unhappy? What are you supposed to do? Just let him do what he likes? You're *grown ups!* You're supposed to know all this stuff. You're supposed to set a good example and I'm not seeing that."

"Lisbet," Pappa warned. "That's quite enough." He stood up and began gathering the plates. "It's time you thought about going back to school tomorrow. Make sure you have your bag packed, ready to go."

Freya watched her sister's reaction.

"What if I'm not well enough to go tomorrow?" Lisbet said, looking straight up at her father fearlessly.

"Well, you seem pretty feisty to me today. So I don't think there will be any excuses in the morning. Understood?"

Lisbet looked down at her empty plate, her face hard as stone.

"Understood?" Pappa repeated quietly.

Lisbet did not make eye contact.

"Yes."

"Lisbet, lille venn, we don't want to force you but the counsellor did say it's best if you can get back to school as soon as possible. Your mind needs distraction," Mamma said.

"What I don't need is all the questions!" Lisbet retorted angrily. "You have no idea, have you? When you've been away from school for even one day, you get mountains of questions. There is no escape."

"Then I'll write a letter," Pappa said firmly. "But you can't stay at home all day every day. It's not good for you."

"How do you know what's good for me?" Lisbet

said defiantly.

Pappa went to Lisbet's chair and pulled it out slowly. Freya held her breath. What was Pappa going to do?

"Stand up please," he said quietly. Lisbet stood, trembling, her eyes locked onto his. Right at that moment she looked frightened and unsure of herself. The hard shell that had been around her suddenly melted. Under Pappa's gaze Lisbet was a little girl again. Then he took her into his big strong arms and she clung to him. He stroked her hair. Said nothing. Mamma sat with her hands in her lap, smiling, with tears in her eyes. Freya looked from one to the other, relieved that Lisbet hadn't pushed Pappa too far.

On Monday morning Freya was surprised to see Lisbet follow her down the stairs into breakfast, rucksack on her back, wearing dark jeans and a dark top. Her hair was tied back smoothly into a ponytail and she was wearing dark eye make-up. Freya stared at her sister's face, trying to get used to this new look. And she was certain Pappa wouldn't like it.

As they sat down to the breakfast table, Pappa came in from the early milking, a deep frown on his face.

"I don't know where that brother of mine is, but I don't appreciate being left to do the entire milking on my own!"

Mamma put a plate of fried eggs in the middle of the table.

"On your own? You mean Felix didn't turn up at all?"

"That's what I said." Pappa sat down and began to butter some toast.

"Coffee?" Mamma said, holding the pot. He nodded and she filled his cup. "Well, did you manage to do it, or do you need me to come back with you after breakfast?"

Pappa shoved a forkful of food into his mouth.

"I think I will need your help, Gretchen. There's mucking out to do. And Snuppen killed three rats last night. I discovered this when I stepped in the leftover gizzards as I came through the door."

"Ew!" Exclaimed Freya, imagining the scene.

Pappa grimaced, then a grin crept through. His gaze flashed over Lisbet's face.

"I like your hair like that, Lisbet. You look pretty today."

Freya's mouth fell open.

Lisbet smirked at her sister, a triumphant look on her face.

"Make sure you get the note from Mamma to give to the teacher," Pappa added.

"Yes, Pappa," said Lisbet.

"And Lisbet?"

"Yes?"

"Be strong and brave today. Don't let their questions get to you. I'm very proud of my girls." He smiled at them both and Freya felt the love in his warm, brown eyes.

Moments later Pappa finished eating, slugged down the rest of his coffee and got to his feet, pushing back his chair.

"Well I'd better get back to the dairy," he said.

"I'll just put these things away and I'll be with you," said Mamma. It all felt so harmonious, a reprieve from the darkness that Freya had felt lingering in every room lately. It firmly pushed the problem back to Onkel Felix and Tante Nina and although that didn't seem fair, in some ways, Freya was relieved. Pappa didn't blame Mamma.

But then he hadn't been injured for life.

CHAPTER TWENTY TWO

At school Freya kept an eye on her sister. Lisbet sat with girls from her class, but didn't really join in the conversation. When they appeared to try and include her, she just smiled wistfully and shook her head or nodded. At least they weren't mean, Freya thought, having expected all sorts of fireworks. Perhaps the teachers of the senior school had warned the students not to ask questions. Freya was relieved. Lisbet had been through enough. Maybe Freya's outburst the other day on her sister's behalf had made an impact? On the long journey home, they both sat reading. Not a single word passed between them, but Freya didn't feel shunned by her sister. She knew the silence was all that was keeping Lisbet together and she didn't want to ruin things for her.

When Freya and Lisbet got home from school that afternoon the house was empty.

"Mamma? Are you here?"

"She's probably at the dairy," said Lisbet, walking upstairs to her room. Freya dumped her bag beside the kitchen table and ran back to the dairy, through the pine trees and turned left up the rocky path to the large red building. The cellar door was wide open and the sound of a radio, faint and tinny, reached her ears. Freya stood for a moment, allowing her eyes to adjust to the dim interior. There was a light switch beside her on the wall. She flicked it on. Mamma was bent over with a shovel in hand, dressed in overalls and gumboots covered in manure.

"Hei Freya! School is over already?" Mamma said.

"Yes, I was wondering where you were and Lisbet said you would probably be in here. Where's Pappa?"

Mamma pointed towards the back of the building.

"He's feeding the calves. Would you like to go and help him?"

"But where's Onkel Felix?"

Mamma frowned.

"He's been gone all day. No one knows where he is." She wiped a hand across her brow. "And it seems he left without taking any of his pain medication with him."

"Poor Tante Nina," Freya said softly. "She must be so worried!"

Mamma gave a rueful smile.

"Why don't you go and help Pappa?" She suggested again. Freya nodded. "And be careful where you walk, lille venn. I haven't finished in here yet."

"I will."

As Freya entered the back room, full of stalls, low steel barricades in which three gangly calves stood separately, she smelled the familiar odour of calf poo. Pappa was working with the smallest, weakest calf, his hand plunged into the bucket of milk while his other hand tried to force the calf's face into it, to encourage it to drink. The little calf was making lots of distressed noises, his huge brown eyes rolling.

"Would you like me to do that, Pappa?" Freya asked.

"Yes, thank you. You're always good with the little ones," Pappa said with relief, stepping out of the stall.

"Onkel Felix has disappeared, Mamma said."

Pappa didn't reply.

"And he left his pain medication behind. He must be really angry," Freya said.

Pappa turned and walked away, saying bitterly,

"It's his choice but I wish he wouldn't leave me with all the work."

Onkel Stefan returned to the house that evening at dinner time and as they all sat down to eat together, the inevitable topic was of course Onkel Felix's disappearance.

"I don't know why he's done this but I wish he'd just grow up!" Onkel Stefan said, frowning.

"He obviously has something he needs to think about," said Mamma diplomatically.

"Why are you so understanding, Gretchen?" Onkel Stefan said. "He's blamed you for years and yet you are still so forgiving." He shook his head. "He doesn't deserve it."

"Stefan," Pappa's tone had a warning in it. He inclined his head towards Freya and Lisbet who had sat completely silent listening to the exchange between the adults with great interest.

"Sorry." Onkel Stefan carved a piece of beef with his knife, smothered it in gravy and chewed with pleasure. "Gretchen, as always, your cooking is marvellous."

"Thank you Stefan," Mamma answered. "You're always so kind to me."

"Well it isn't exactly difficult," he said with a smile. Even Pappa had to chuckle at that.

The conversation remained jovial and light until the girls were sent to bed. But as Freya later sat on the tenth step listening to the adults talking in the kitchen, she heard a different story.

"Well, I think we should search the island first," suggested Onkel Stefan. "I'll take the blueberry wood, our beach and that place where we used to pick hazelnuts."

"Good," Pappa answered. "I'll check the church and the ferry wharf to see if he's taken the ferry today."

"I wonder if he took Bestefar's boat?" Said Mamma. "In that case he could be anywhere."

"Well," Pappa answered. "We should check all the places we used to go as children first, just in case his holed up there, feeling sorry for himself." It was unusual to hear Pappa sounding annoyed.

"I'm just worried what he'll do!" said Mamma, her voice pitched high and wavering. A moment's silence followed. Freya's brain raced. What did Mamma mean by that?

"Hopefully it won't come to that," Pappa reassured her.

"Yes," Onkel Stefan agreed. "Hopefully he'll see sense and come home."

"Poor Nina. She must be worried sick!" exclaimed Mamma.

"We'll find him, Gretchen," said Onkel Stefan. "I'll drag him home by the ear if I have to."

"He can be very strong," Mamma said, worriedly.

Onkel Stefan chuckled.

"But I have a few years on him. And no dodgy leg."

"Let's not get carried away," warned Pappa. "A systematic search and I'm sure we'll find him. Now, how about another coffee Stefan?" And with that the conversation soon became boring to Freya. She yawned and crept back up the stairs to her bed. But she lay awake, hands behind her head, thinking about Onkel Felix. What if he had some sort of accident and drowned? They'd never find him in the fjord. Only the fish would… Freya sat bolt upright. Lorelei! Tomorrow she would ask for her secret friend's help.

CHAPTER TWENTY THREE

At six in the morning Freya was down by the shore sitting on her favourite rock and singing to call Lorelei. The sky was grey. Thick granite coloured scudded overhead, pushed by an urgent wind. Choppy waves splashed on the rocks, spraying Freya's bare legs with icy water. Lorelei must have been nearby for she responded quickly to Freya's song. Gliding smoothly through the water she emerged onto her rock and sat, double blinking at Freya.

"Good morning Lorelei," Freya said. "It's a school day and I've got something very important to ask you." Freya shifted her position so that she could lean closer to the havfrue. "Have you seen Onkel Felix? You know, my uncle with the bad leg?" Freya tapped her leg and winced as if she was in pain. Lorelei watched her closely, her large eyes moving from Freya's face to her leg and back to her face again. She made a chittering sound, the tiny sharp points of her teeth appearing behind her lips. Freya got up and mimed walking with a bad leg.

"Onkel Felix?" She pointed to the water and mimed rowing in a boat. Lorelei looked from Freya to the water and back to Freya and made the chittering sound once more. "I'm really worried!" Freya rubbed her temples. "I hardly got any sleep last night. But poor Tante Nina - she hasn't been well lately. And now this. And the baby too, you know?" Freya sighed, watching Lorelei's face for any sign of understanding.

"Squawk!" Lorelei said, nodding vigorously, staring at Freya's face. "Squawk, squawk!" She slapped her lower body.

"Yes! Yes, that's him!" Freya felt excitement building inside her chest. Lorelei understood! "Have you seen him?" She pointed at the fjord, miming him falling overboard, swimming badly, struggling in the water.

Lorelei watched her very closely, blinking rapidly. She slapped her chest with both hands and then reached out to Freya entreatingly. A whining sound came from her lips, something Freya had never heard before. There was such sadness in the sound, such longing.

"Yes, I'm worried. You understand that don't you?"

Lorelei moaned and held out her hands to Freya. Freya got to her feet and walked carefully over the stones until she reached the havfrue's side. She held out her hands and Lorelei took them both, squeezing hard and pulling Freya close. Their faces were inches apart as Lorelei chittered anxiously. Freya swallowed and blinked, quite overwhelmed by Lorelei's breath, staring at the havfrue's strange but beautiful eyes, curved like glass balls, in which she could see her own face reflected.

"Yes, you do understand, don't you?" Freya said softly. "You're my best friend in the *whole world*." She sighed. "I need your help, Lorelei. Would you go and search for him, please? Onkel Felix?" She pulled a hand free of Lorelei's grasp and slapped her thigh again. "The man," she put her hand up high to indicate how tall he was. "With the bad leg," she slapped her thigh again. Then she pointed at the fjord. "You go? Go search?"

Lorelei barked; a harsh sound that almost hurt Freya's ears. Then she slithered off the rock, swallowed by the churning waters without even a splash from her tail. Freya made herself comfortable on her own rock, which was damp and cold and wished she had brought a blanket or something warm to wrap around herself.

Moments passed. Freya jigged her foot trying to keep warm, and scanned the fjord for any sign of Lorelei. Turning briefly to look at her home she saw the lights were on downstairs which meant Mamma was up and making breakfast. There wasn't much time left before Freya had to leave for the bus.

"Come on Lorelei," she whispered. "Please find him."

Suddenly, Lorelei's face broke the surface. She pulled herself up onto the rock with one hand. In the other hand she clasped something to her chest.

"What is it? What is it Lorelei?" Freya asked anxiously, thinking to see some small object belonging to her uncle. Dreading the thought of what might have happened, but needing desperately to know. Lorelei opened her long fingered hand. On her palm rested a tiny fish, still alive. The havfrue chittered excitedly to Freya, her head bobbing, her eyes double blinking repeatedly.

"Oh," Freya said, disappointed. She shook her head. "No, that's not what I meant." Lorelei shifted on her rock, reaching out to Freya, holding the wriggling little fish by the tail, chittering. "No that's not it!" Freya shook her head and folded her arms.

Lorelei grunted, then popped the fish into her mouth and slid back into the water. Moments later she reappeared, right at Freya's feet. Her sleek, long hair streamed down her back, her thin, muscular arm reaching out to Freya. This time she offered a beautiful shell with patterns that looked as if they'd been hand painted. She chittered excitedly waving the shell front of Freya's face. Freya took the offering and tried to smile.

"Thank you. It's beautiful. But Onkel Felix? Where is he?"

Lorelei's head tilted to one side as she double blinked at Freya.

"You don't understand, do you?" Freya said softly. She let out a deep sigh. "I should never have asked you to help. We can't even speak the same language." She turned her head away from the havfrue. All the misery of Lisbet's secret, the joy of Tante Nina's new baby, and the fear and dread of what had happened to Onkel Felix bubbled up inside Freya until she couldn't control it any longer. She started to cry, feeling helpless. Wiping her dripping nose on her sleeve, Freya looked at her havfrue friend, who lay half submerged in the water staring up at Freya's face, her mouth half open, her strange eyes watching intently. Lorelei reached out a cold, clammy fingertip and dabbed at the tears on Freya's cheek, then sucked her finger. A deep noise resonated in Lorelei's throat. Freya patted Lorelei's hand and got to her feet.

"I have to go. I need to have breakfast and go to school. But I hope that I'll see you this afternoon? Maybe then you'll have some news for me."

Clutching the beautiful shell Lorelei gave her, Freya trudged slowly up the slope to Fjellheim, wondering where Onkel Felix had spent the night. His leg must hurt badly now, after a whole day without medicine.

But just how long would his anger keep him from his wife and unborn child?

CHAPTER TWENTY FOUR

The sun was shining warm as Freya arrived at school that day. Lisbet wordlessly went over to the senior school building without a backward glance. The primary school children raced about the playground, a rainbow of darting colour as they squealed and laughed. The bitumen was still damp with last night's light rain and smelled faintly of tar. Along the outer edge of the school grounds trees were in full pink blossom, shedding pink snow over the wooden benches. Freya breathed in deep as she walked through the school gate, relieved to be away from the sadness and worry at home. Then a figure caught her eye. At last, Britt was back at school! Freya rushed over, backpack bouncing, and hugged her.

"Hei!" Freya cried joyfully.

"Hei," replied Britt, pushing her dark, straight hair from her blue eyes. She had an impish face, with a freckled nose the boys loved to tease her about. But Britt didn't care. She was one of those kids who didn't mind much what others thought of her. She knew what she liked and what she didn't. Britt was in general a quiet girl, but occasionally spoke her mind, which would surprise people. You could see it on their faces. Especially the boys who thought to tease her. She was a farm girl, used to hard work, dealing with sick and injured animals and this gave her confidence most of the town children didn't possess. She also had three brothers, so the bullies in their class made no impact on her. One day, to everyone's astonishment, she punched a boy in the nose after he deliberately tripped her up and laughed at her as she fell onto bare knees on the bitumen. Her face red with anger, Britt gave Rune no time to think. Her fist lashed out, quick as a snake and everyone just stood there, mouths open. Until Freya whooped and started clapping.

Later in class, Mrs Lindstrøm tried to look stern, but when she heard the same account from several students she concluded Rune had earned it and nothing more was said about the matter. Since then the boys had given Britt no trouble, apart from the occasional mention of her freckles. Britt was a great friend to have because all she had to do was stare hard at a boy and he backed off. And not just the boys either. The snooty girls left them mostly alone. Freya loved Britt's confidence. It was just a shame she was so often away from school. When asked about this, the answer was always the same – she'd had a cold. Freya had invited Britt home for a weekend visit once, but Britt had said she couldn't leave home for even one night. It was disappointing, but what could you do? Friends like Britt were rare, so you were just glad for the times you had together and missed them when they weren't around.

Britt had been away for a couple of weeks now, so there was a lot to catch up on.

"So, how is everything?" Freya asked, as they hung their bags up on the hooks and went back outside to play on the swings.

"Good. Had a bad cold. You know," Britt said vaguely, bending down to tie up her shoelace.

"It's so good to see you back though!" Enthused Freya. "I've missed you. Hey, and guess what? Tante Nina is pregnant!"

"Wow! A cousin!" said Britt, smiling up at her. "I've got seven cousins, you know." She straightened and they continued outside.

"Yeah, well this is my first," replied Freya. "And it will be a lot younger than me and Lisbet."

Britt shook her head.

"That doesn't matter. You'll still have loads of fun. Babies are soooo cute! I got to change my little cousin Randi's nappy once."

Freya pulled a face, imagining the stink.

Britt collapsed into laughter.

"Your face! You should see it! No, it wasn't that bad. A, er, number one, I suppose you could say."

"Oh," Freya said, giggling. "You know what I was thinking."

"You're so funny Freya!" She nudged her friend. Freya nudged her back. They toppled towards the swings laughing. "Push me first?" Asked Britt.

"Sure."

"So, what else has been happening while I've been away?" Britt asked, extending her legs and leaning back as she soared through the air. "Wee! Higher, Freya!"

"Well," huffed Freya, thinking to tell the even more exciting news about Lorelei. But then changed her mind. "Oh, not much."

Britt twisted her head to look as far back towards Freya as she could.

"Not much? Weren't you just going to tell me something? Come on!"

"Well. Oof!" Freya pushed Britt hard, making her squeal again. She watched her friend's back coming towards her, Britt's shaggy dark hair blowing in the breeze. She pushed again.

"You don't have to tell me if you don't want to," said Britt, leaning back and looking at Freya upside down. She giggled. "Secrets are good, you know. You don't have to share all of them. Some are good to keep just for you."

Freya pushed Britt a little softer and said nothing. She was thinking about Onkel Felix. Where was he? Trapped somewhere? Drowned? Would Tante Nina's baby come out fatherless?

"Hey, Freya," Britt said softly. Freya felt a gentle pressure on her shoulder and looked up. Britt was standing in front of her, peering into her face. "What's wrong?"

Freya felt her face grow hot and turned away. She walked to the benches surrounded by pink blossom and sat down. Britt sat next to her. All around them the other children shrieked and laughed and ran everywhere at full speed, like frantic bees gathering nectar before a storm;

for the school bell was about to ring.

Freya took a deep breath and twisted her fingers together.

"My Onkel Felix has gone missing."

"Missing? When?"

"Since yesterday morning. No one knows where he is. And he could be hurt. He forgot his pain medication. And his bad leg is probably in agony by now." Freya heard Britt's exhale.

"Hm. That doesn't sound good. Why did he go? Did he run away?"

"Sort of," replied Freya. She looked up at the road outside the school where cars flashed by, their bright paint colours and chrome side mirrors catching the sunlight. "He's always upset, or angry at Mamma. But this time he was angry at Onkel Stefan. And that doesn't even make sense." Freya bit her lip.

"Onkel Stefan? I didn't know you had another uncle."

"He's the youngest." Freya turned to her friend and smiled shyly. "He's lots of fun. He isn't married. And he's got lots of funny stories. And he can pick me up and twirl me around as if I weighed nothing."

Britt looked impressed.

"He must be pretty strong. My dad doesn't pick me up anymore. He says I'm way too heavy. And Mamma says young ladies don't do that sort of thing."

"That's a shame," said Freya. "It's so much fun!"

"You're lucky," observed Britt. "But I DO have three annoying brothers," she said with mock seriousness.

"Better than a moody older sister," said Freya,

darkly.

Britt laughed.

"Nothing makes you happy, does it?"

"What do you mean?" Freya said, her words tangled in a laugh. A vision of Lorelei slopping milk all over herself sprang to Freya's mind and she covered her mouth to stifle further giggles.

"What?"

"Nothing."

"What is it? Come on. Tell me!"

Freya got her face under control.

"It's nothing."

"Yes it is!"

The bell rang and they made their way to ingangen - a room lined with pale, fragrant wood, where they removed their shoes and placed them side by side on the rack.

"Come on Freya." Britt jumped in front of her friend and grabbed her shoulders. Peering into her face she said seriously, "I can see you want to tell me. Look into my eyes... It's my secret power..."

Freya shoved her gently aside and laughed.

"Stop that. You're making me laugh so hard I'm going to choke."

"Ha ha! Good." Britt walked ahead to their desks where they sat side by side. Freya hoped Britt wouldn't get them into trouble today because the first thing Mrs Lindstrøm did was separate them and last time Freya had ended up sitting next to Tommy Nygård – the naughtiest boy in the class.

CHAPTER TWENTY FIVE

It was the most perfect ferry ride Freya could remember. The sun shone brilliantly, sparkling off the dark green water as the small ferry cut through it like a knife, the ripples fanning out from the bow. The sky was the deepest most beautiful blue, fading to the horizon. Dark, jagged peaks in the distance still had a smattering of snow in their deep crevices, but the lower slopes were green with the newness of spring. Freya stood at the front, just tall enough to put her elbows on top of the metal sides of the open deck. As the ferry made its squiggly way through outcrops and tiny islets, Freya saw waterbirds feeding, while their grey and white fluffy chicks waited in rocky nests nearby, bright orange beaks open, hungry. The wind was gentle, ruffling her hair and as she turned her face towards the sun, a shadow came across her vision. To her amazement, a *havørn*, sea eagle, hovered right above where she stood, gliding on the warm winds above the ferry, its cream coloured tail fanned out and graceful, brown, speckled wings spread wide. Her breath held in wonder, Freya squinted up at its fierce face and marvelled at its beauty, the curved yellow beak, the dark eyes scanning for prey. For a moment she considered running downstairs to fetch Lisbet, but something told her by the time they came back the eagle, and the moment, would be gone.

Suddenly the havørn fell back a little, veering swiftly away from the ferry, having spotted its prey. Freya smiled, feeling lucky to have seen such a beautiful creature up close.

All too soon the ferry reached Eikeberg, the ramp clanked down to meet the wharf and the cars drove slowly off. The minibus waited to take the girls home, while a couple of cars lined up to take the late afternoon ferry into town. As Freya walked past Ragnar, toiling with the large rope, he called out to her.

"*Ha det*, (bye) Freya!"

She waved at him and smiled, and was so busy watching what he was doing that she tripped and almost fell flat on her face. A hand grabbed her backpack and pulled her backwards.

"Careful!" Lisbet said from behind her.

Freya turned and smiled sheepishly at her sister.

"Thanks, Lisbet. I was so busy watching Ragnar I wasn't looking where I was going."

Lisbet's mouth pressed into a very thin line and colour came to her cheeks, but she said nothing and walked stiffly towards the minibus. What had Freya done now to upset her sister? She turned back to glimpse the deckhand again but he was busy getting ready for the next load of cars.

When they arrived home they were surprised to see snowy-haired Gamle Jenny sitting at the kitchen table, wearing Mamma's red spotted apron over her plain blue dress. A plate of fresh-baked cookies sat on the table, the aroma of vanilla filling the warm kitchen. A delicate cup and saucer sat between the old lady's hands.

"Where's Mamma?" Freya asked, worriedly, as she slung her schoolbag down on the floor next to a kitchen chair. "Is she alright?"

"She's fine," Gamle Jenny nodded, with an unconvincing half-smile. "She doesn't want you to worry, but they had to go to town rather quickly."

"Something wrong?" Lisbet said, frowning.

"It's your Tante Nina," Gamle Jenny answered quietly, her pale blue eyes calm.

"Tante Nina!" Freya cried. "Is the baby okay?"

"Now, girls, sit down with me for a minute and I will explain." Gamle Jenny pushed the plate of cookies closer.

Freya sat down but Lisbet stood resolutely by the table, watching Gamle Jenny.

"Tante Nina needed to go to the hospital, so your parents went with her," the old lady explained.

"But why did Pappa have to go too?" Freya asked.

"Your Onkel Felix still hasn't returned, so your father was going to look for him on the mainland."

"Onkel Stefan isn't back yet?"

"No. Sorry," Gamle Jenny answered.

"So the cows will just milk themselves then," Lisbet said without emotion.

"That won't be necessary. Mrs Vestad's grandson is visiting her at the moment and he has worked on dairies before," said Gamle Jenny. "Fortunately, he was here at just the right time and agreed to help out. Now, how about a cookie?"

Freya looked at the plate of pale cookies, with their crunchy edges and tiny chips of chocolate melted into them. They did smell delicious.

"*Tusen takk.*"

"Yeah, very thoughtful of you. Takk," Lisbet said and left the room to go upstairs.

"Lisbet, are you sure you're not hungry?" Gamle Jenny called out, but there was no reply.

"Can I have some milk too?" Freya asked.

"Certainly," Gamle Jenny said. "Help yourself. So how was school today?"

"It was great!" Freya said pouring some milk into a glass and putting the bottle back in the fridge. "Britt came back, which was fantastic. I really missed her when she was away." Freya savoured the taste of the melting chocolate on her tongue, then a sip of creamy milk. "Is Tante Nina really okay? She's not going to lose the baby is she? What happened?"

"I'm not sure how much to tell you," Gamle Jenny admitted. "But perhaps you do need to know that she started bleeding a little. And sometimes that can be a bad sign. But not always," She hastened to add, holding up a finger. But it was obvious from her worried expression that Gamle Jenny was indeed concerned.

"When will they be back?" Freya asked.

Gamle Jenny shook her head.

"I'm not sure. But I'll be here. I'll cook you a

delicious dinner and we'll watch TV together. How does that sound?"

"Can we watch my favourite show?" Freya asked.

"Of course. That will be fun, won't it?" Gamle Jenny smiled. Then her face turned sombre. "How is Lisbet these days?"

Freya shrugged and took a second cookie.

"She doesn't talk to me much. Something is definitely bothering her but she says she can't tell anyone. Not just yet anyway. But today she seemed really sad." Freya paused, thinking back to the ferry ride. "It was such fantastic weather this afternoon on the ferry, and I saw a havørn, gliding right above me! But Lisbet stayed downstairs. I wish I knew what was making her so unhappy."

Gamle Jenny sat quietly, her sun-spotted, old hands fiddling with a tea towel.

"I'm sure she will tell us when she is ready," the old lady said softly. As if on cue, Lisbet walked through the kitchen and out the back door without a word. Freya and Gamle Jenny looked at each other and shrugged.

"Maybe she just wants to be outside, because it's so sunny," Freya offered.

"Maybe," Gamle Jenny said.

"I think I'll go and see where she is."

"Make sure you change into your play clothes first."

Ten minutes later Freya came down the stairs again. She had been side tracked by her journal lying open on her bed and decided to write a few lines before she went outside. As she closed the back door behind her, Freya felt the breeze freshening and all the subtle fragrances of spring wash over her - the pale pink of cherry blossom, the vibrant green of the grass. Small, pale yellow polyanthus that Bestemor Hilde had planted many years ago carpeted the lawn. As she set off down the slope towards the shoreline, Freya scanned the water automatically for signs of Lorelei, but instead of the tiny splash of a mermaid's tail she saw her sister, out in Bestefar's boat, rowing frantically towards the middle of the fjord.

Freya cupped her hands around her mouth.

"Lisbet! Lisbet, what are you doing?" Running down the slope, she tripped on a grass tussock and fell heavily on one knee. Limping down to the shore, Freya kept her eyes fixed on the tiny red figure in the small green boat, feeling a lump of terror in her throat. The sun shone on Lisbet's fair hair like pure gold. But she was now too far away to hear her sister's frantic calls. Freya climbed up onto the tallest rock and waved her arms trying to catch Lisbet's attention.

Then she saw something that made her heart fly up into her mouth. A speedboat, with a water skier attached, was heading from the west, around the curve of a large islet, a white churning wake following it, heading straight for Lisbet. The force of the waves rippling out from the motor boat could easily capsize Bestefar's little green row boat. As the skier slid by Lisbet, he took one hand off the handle bar and waved merrily. Lisbet clung to the oars as the wake from the motor boat jostled her. The waves grew larger. Lisbet dropped the oars and clutched the side of the boat with both hands. Alarmingly, the boat tipped right, tipped left, then tipped right and with one swift movement, Lisbet lost her hold and slid into the churning water like a dead fish.

Too shocked to even cry out, Freya waited for a spluttering, arm-waving figure to surface, splashing about and trying to grab onto the boat. But there was no splashing. The boat had righted itself and sat bobbing quite happily as the ripples receded and the sound of the engine died away. There was still no sign of Lisbet. Freya stood, helpless on the shore, her mind churning at full speed. There was no time to fetch Gamle Jenny, no time to telephone someone. Mamma and Pappa were in town with Tante Nina. And who knew where Onkel Stefan might be. Lisbet was drowning, right now, and there was only one person who could help.

"Lorelei!" screamed Freya. "Lorelei, help!"

But shouting had never brought the havfrue to the shore. And Freya had to calm herself, to think. *Sing!* Freya's voice wavered, her eyes still fixed on the spot where Lisbet had slipped beneath the waves. She sang as loud as she could, searching, searching for Lorelei. But there was no sign of either. By the time she had sung the first and second verses and was onto another round of the chorus Freya's voice was a screech.

A small splash and the flip of a frilly tail broke the surface.

"Lorelei! Help!" Freya screamed.

With effortless grace, Lorelei surfaced and pulled her smooth, grey-green body up onto her usual rock, regarding Freya with her strange, serene eyes.

"Lorelei! You have to help! Lisbet is drowning! There, over there!" Freya pointed a trembling arm at the bobbing boat.

Lorelei chittered, unconcerned, plucking at bits of

seaweed stuck in her hair.

"Please, help my sister!" Freya ran into the water, her jeans and shoes instantly soaked. She beckoned Lorelei to follow, pointing to the boat.

"Come! Come and find Lisbet!"

Lorelei spread her glistening hair over her shoulders to dry in the sun and leaned back on her hands.

"No, no, Lorelei!" Freya scrambled over the rocks and grabbed Lorelei's arm, yanking her towards the water. Lorelei screeched in alarm, her eyes double blinking rapidly. Freya let go and ran to the shallows.

"Come on!" Freya cried, beckoning desperately.

Lorelei chittered again, and finally saw the boat out in the middle of the fjord.

"Yes! Yes, that's it Lorelei. Lisbet… " Freya nodded vigorously, pointing at the boat.

Lorelei tilted her head and stared at Freya, searching the girl's face. Freya felt caught in a spell, a spell of waiting for Lorelei to understand.

In a flash, Lorelei slipped into the sea.

"Oh!" Freya cried, watching the waves. There! Lorelei's head popped up, then disappeared again. Freya dried her nose on her sleeve, feeling hopeful. Lorelei would find Lisbet. A slight breeze had pushed the boat away from where Lisbet had fallen in, but that wouldn't matter would it? Lorelei could see clearly under water. She was a princess of the sea. Nothing escaped her notice. Freya waited, and her confidence faltered. Was it so dark in the fjord she couldn't see? Was Lisbet already dead? Had the havfrue lost interest and swum away?

Her teeth chattering with the cold, Freya came to a brave decision, inspired by an old story of her father and his brothers, an emergency, right here on this island. She stripped off her wet jeans, socks and shoes until she was wearing only her underpants and a T-shirt. Plunging into the frigid water she gasped in shock. At first her strokes were strong and as she calmed her breathing Freya began to hope. But, stroke after stroke, she began to tire very quickly. It felt like two strong men were pulling her arms down. Her chest ached, every breath a sharp agony. Still, she kicked and forced her arms to lift into the air, to push through the water, to lift again, keeping her eyes on the point between the shore and Bollen where Lisbet had fallen in.

CHAPTER TWENTY SIX

Little waves splashed into her eyes and down her throat, the salty water making her feel sick. Her legs kicked erratically, with no rhythm. She was growing weaker. In front of her Bollen rose, straight up out of the fjord, as if to say: I am here. I will be your guide. Somewhere between herself and that mountain Lisbet lay in the embrace of the dark fjord. And a havfrue searched.

Suddenly, Lorelei surfaced, an unconscious girl held in her strong arms. Lisbet's head lolled to the side, her lips parted, her eyes closed.

"Lisbet!" Freya tried to shout, but what came out was a gurgle as water slopped into her mouth. She spluttered, coughed and tried again. "Bring her here! Bring her here, Lorelei!" The havfrue, suspended effortlessly in the water, regarded Freya with a calm, cold expression. Her large, wide eyes double blinked slowly, the inside lids swept from the outside and in, then the over lids swept down and up again. Meanwhile Freya struggled to stay afloat, her legs weakly kicking, her chin just barely above water.

"Please, Lorelei, bring Lisbet to the shore. Thank you so much for finding her!"

And then, as Freya watched in horror, Lorelei sank below the surface taking Lisbet with her.

Freya gurgle-screamed, kicking, thrashing her arms, her breath strangled in her throat. Spinning round to look at the shore she saw what she'd known in her heart she would see - no one. No one even knew that her sister, Lisbet, was gone forever. The cold was biting into her face as with a desperate last effort, Freya began to struggle towards the shore.

The sound of a small motor, like an angry bee, drifted across the fjord. But Freya didn't even have the strength to turn and look. And it was probably too far away to help anyhow. They'd never see her tiny head in the water. The motor grew louder. Closer. Gasping, Freya spun. Hope flared again. The little boat was speeding towards her. In it sat a man leaning forward, one hand on the tiller the other shading his eyes. He called out.

"Freya, is that you?"

"Onkel Felix!" Freya cried weakly. "Lisbet..." Her legs suddenly turned to jelly and she began to sink. She just had no energy left to fight. Then a thought flashed inside her brain. *Float on your back when you get tired.* Slowly she rolled over onto her back, her face towards the blue, blue sky, so serene in its ignorance of the tragedy happening down below it. The motor died as the boat glided towards her. Strong arms lifted her high and into the boat. She turned to cling to her uncle, shivering so hard her teeth rattled together.

"Put your arms up. Put your arms up, lille venn," he said, urgently.

She obeyed and a warm, fleecy jumper slid over her body.

"What's happened? Why are you out here in the fjord?"

Freya fought not to cry. Tears would not help right now.

"Lisbet... Bestefar's boat...speedboat... fell in..." Freya gushed all in one breath. She took another. "And Lorelei has taken her down to the deep!"

"Lorelei?" he said, confused, pushing his dark hair out of his eyes.

"Yes, my friend, the havfrue!" Freya sobbed, heartbroken. "I should have listened to Gamle Jenny! I should have listened! Now Lisbet is dead and it's all my fault!"

"Where? Where exactly did she fall in?" Onkel Felix demanded, gripping Freya's shoulders. "Freya, where did she fall in?"

"I don't know!" Freya sobbed. "It's too late."

"No, there's still a chance, Freya! Where?"

Freya looked up into his face. Gone was the anger, the pain, the sneer. He was a different man - calm, compassionate, determined. His dark eyes flashed bright with worry. She pointed at the spot in the water. Without a word, Onkel Felix dived over the side of the boat, fully clothed. Freya clapped a hand over her mouth in dismay.

"Not you too..." She whispered. "Please, not both

of you!" Freya scanned the shore, hoping to see Gamle Jenny on the verandah, or making her slow way down the slope. But the house sat placidly as usual in the afternoon sun, the verandah empty. Turning back to the water Freya saw bubbles rising to the surface. She sat up straighter. Two heads appeared, two sets of hands tearing at each other, two faces snarling - Onkel Felix and Lorelei. A third head rose - a limp, unconscious girl, gripped around her chest by the havfrue's long, muscular arm. Onkel Felix struggled to wrestle his niece from the havfrue's grasp. He yelled, pushing his feet against Lorelei's mighty chest, trying to get his hands around Lisbet. Freya could only watch, her breath caught in her throat, her heart thudding so hard in her chest she thought she was going to faint. Noise boomed in her ears, like the din and crash of waves smashing into the shore on a stormy night.

"Argh!" Onkel Felix growled and with a final push, wrenched Lisbet from the havfrue's arms. A wild animal's screech rent the air. Lorelei's eyes were black with hatred, her pointy teeth crashed together with rage. In vain, she tried to take Lisbet's body from Onkel Felix but he was kicking at her, struggling closer to the boat.

"Freya!" He gasped, his black hair plastered to his head. "Help me get Lisbet onboard!"

One of Lisbet's hands and one foot were flung over the side of the boat. Freya grabbed first one then the other and pulled with all her might. A choked scream issued from Lisbet's mouth as her body was pushed and hauled over the hard wooden edge. Onkel Felix gave one final grunt and Lisbet slumped sideways onto the floor of the boat, her eyes closed, water pouring out of her mouth.

"Lisbet!" Freya screamed. "Lisbet…" She pushed the sodden hair away from her sister's face. Lisbet moaned but her eyes remained closed. "Oh! You're alive! Lisbet, wake-up! Onkel Felix, she won't wake up!" Freya cried, looking round for her uncle, expecting him to be climbing into the boat.

But there was no sign of him.

And there was no sign of Lorelei.

CHAPTER TWENTY SEVEN

Freya peered into her sister's face.

"Lisbet, wake up!" Freya sat back on her haunches in the small motorboat. Lisbet was alive. It was a start. And now, somehow, Freya had to get her sister up to Fjellheim to warmth and safety. Tearfully, Freya scanned once more for signs of Onkel Felix in the water.

Nothing.

Shivering, Freya stood and reached out to steady herself as she stumbled to the stern where the small motor hung over the transept. She had never started a motorboat before, but had watched her father and uncle many times. Gripping the T shaped handle of the rip cord she braced one foot against the boat and pulled as hard as she could. The motor spluttered, then died. Biting her lip, Freya pulled again. The motor roared and settled to a low grumbling. Now she had to figure out how to get it into forward gear. Freya finally discovered a lever, labelled F and B, *Foran* and *Bak*. She pushed it towards F and with a lurch, the boat surged straight out towards the middle of the fjord. Gripping the tiller Freya sat down and steered it in a wide arc, back towards shore.

As she approached the rocks, Freya cut the motor and let the boat glide in, as she had seen Pappa do so many times. For a tiny moment Freya felt proud of herself. Jumping out she yanked on the boat, trying to haul it up the ramp in front of Fjellheim. But her arms were too thin and weak. She rushed to Lisbet, grabbed her sister's arms and tried to haul her out of the boat. But an unconscious sixteen-year-old girl was a deadweight, far too heavy for a girl of twelve. Frantically, Freya tugged on the boat once more and managed to pull it up an inch. The tide was flowing out, away from the boat. Lisbet would be safe for a while.

Every breath like cold fire in her chest, Freya forced her legs to pump, up the slope towards the house. She kept her head down and focused on each exhausted step, her bare feet slipping on the new green grass. By the time she got to the back door her legs crumpled beneath her. Weakly, she banged on the door. There was no response. Her cold, numb fingers managed to turn the doorknob and she hauled herself in through the doorway to collapse on the floor.

"Freya!" Gamle Jenny exclaimed. A chair scraped on the floor. Warm hands touched Freya's face.

"Lis… Help…" Freya cried feebly, gasping for a breath so tiny it wouldn't have been enough for a sparrow.

"Where's your puffer?" Gamle Jenny said sharply.

"Kitchen... drawer..." Freya whispered, her breath whining in her throat, her head dizzy and thick. The puffer was shaken vigorously and thrust into her hand. Freya managed to sit up and breathed in the Ventolin. A soft, wool blanket settled around her shoulders. A warm towel dried her hair.

"What are you doing?" Freya screeched, clutching the old lady's leg. "We have to help Lisbet!"

"Where? Where is she?" Gamle Jenny said, struggling to bend her old knees to crouch beside Freya. Her silver white hair and worried blue eyes came into Freya's view.

"Bestefar's boat. Down at the..." Freya's words were snatched away by a coughing fit. She heard footsteps leave and the back door slam. Freya lay on her back on the floor and waited for her breathing to ease. A thought crashed into her head as she lay there. She had to telephone for help! Freya forced herself up and stumbled to the telephone, which sat on a dresser in the hall at the foot of the stairs. Her numb fingers flicked through the wafer thin pages of the phone book, but in her hurry and distress she couldn't find the name of the hospital. Rushing to the front door she peered through the glass. Down by the shore the old lady wrestled to pull Lisbet from the boat. Turning back to the phone book Freya paused for a moment and tried to think. Emergency numbers... At the front. She dialled.

"Strandafjord Regional Hospital, how may I help you?" A woman's voice answered.

"My sister, she's almost drowned. She needs help!"

"Who is this?"

"Freya Askvold."

"What is your emergency?"

"My sister almost drowned! She's unconscious. My parents are at the hospital with Tante Nina. I don't know what to do!"

"How old are you?"

"I'm twelve. Why does that matter? You have to help me!"

"What was your name again?"

"FREYA ASKVOLD!" Freya screamed. "Why are you asking me again? Help me!"

"No need to shout, dear." The lady replied calmly.

"Why aren't you listening to me?" Freya screeched, sobbing.

"Your parents' names?" The woman said snippily.

"Torstein and Gretchen Askvold. Hurry! My sister Lisbet…"

"Do you require an ambulance?"

"Yes!"

"What is your address?"

"Fjellheim, Askvold Dairy, Eikeberg," Freya answered, wiping her nose on the blanket. "How long will it take to get here?"

"To Eikeberg? I don't know. When's the next ferry?"

"I don't know! I'm just a kid. Will you please tell my parents!" Freya was so disheartened she dropped the phone and slumped to the floor. She had reached the end of her strength. She could do no more.

CHAPTER TWENTY EIGHT

Within ten minutes Lisbet was rugged up in bed with an electric blanket switched to high. Gamle Jenny came into the room and handed a pink towel to Freya.

"Dry her hair, lille venn. She is too weak to do it."

It seemed strange to be touching Lisbet so closely, to smell her clean skin and golden hair. Lisbet's lashes were so fine and blonde, like a fairy's. Her breathing was slow and calm. Freya tried to be as gentle as possible. Now and then Lisbet would open her bloodshot eyes slowly and smile at her sister, then fall back to exhausted sleep.

There was a commotion downstairs. Voices in the kitchen. Footsteps tramped up the stairs and a man and woman dressed in paramedic uniforms of pale blue trousers and white shirts entered Lisbet's room. The man was so tall he had to bend forward to clear the doorway.

On his collared shirt was a badge that read 'Jens'. The woman's badge read 'Monika'. She opened a medical bag and sat on Lisbet's bed to take her pulse while Jens wrapped a wide band around Lisbet's arm to take her blood pressure. Then Monika popped a thermometer in Lisbet's mouth and smiled at her.

"You are a very lucky girl, I hear," she said.

Lisbet smiled lopsidedly with the thermometer under her tongue.

"Your uncle saved you, I believe?" Jens said, gently pulling Lisbet forward to a sitting position. "And your little sister was a bit of a hero too." He placed a stethoscope on her back, then listened carefully.

"Does she have pneumonia?" Freya asked anxiously. "Could she…?"

Jens pulled away, gently laying Lisbet against the soft pillows.

"She's fine. She has a strong heart and her lungs are pretty clear, considering what she's just been through." He turned to Gamle Jenny. "Normally we'd keep her in hospital for a couple of days, but she seems fine here. As long as you monitor her temperature every hour." He crouched in front of Freya. "Do you think you could do that for your sister?"

Freya looked into his kind eyes and nodded.

"What about Onkel Felix?" She asked, feeling the black fear and cold of the fjord rise up to her throat. "Can you help us look for him?" He looked away to his companion. Monika shook her head sadly. Freya clutched Jens' white shirt. "Please! He saved her and he needs help!"

Jens stood and looked down at her. He looked

again at Monika and shrugged.

"All right. Let's go." He took Freya's hand. "Show me where you saw him last."

Without a word Freya dragged him downstairs. Just as they reached the kitchen door it opened. Mamma and Pappa were home. From the looks on their faces the hospital had passed on Freya's message.

"Lisbet?" Mamma's deep blue eyes were huge with worry as she sought Gamle Jenny's response. The old lady laid a hand on Mamma's arm.

"Hush, she is fine. Upstairs. The medics said she could stay here."

"I must see her!" Mamma rushed towards the stairs.

"But Mamma, Onkel Felix is missing! We're going down to the shore to find Onkel Felix!" Freya cried out.

Mamma turned.

"I'll be with you in a minute."

"And I'll stay with Lisbet," Gamle Jenny said. "They'll need you down there, Gretchen."

It was a large group that tramped down the slope from Fjellheim to the shore. Mamma had grabbed her warm navy parka to wear over her brightly coloured dress and ran after them to catch up, grabbing Pappa's hand. Pappa pulled his cap down firmly over his forehead, his eyes scanning the water with a deep furrowed frown. Freya had for once thought to put on her gumboots. The medics Jens and Monika took long, determined strides, which gave Freya hope. Onkel Felix's boat sat half beached on the rocks where Freya had left it. Lisbet's red jumper lay in the shallows. Pulling the sodden garment up Freya handed it to Mamma who wrung it out with her strong hands. Bestefar's little row boat had been carried by the tide far out into the fjord. It was now a tiny green speck against the darker ocean green. Freya pointed in line with Bollen.

"There. That's where Lisbet fell in. That's where Onkel Felix fought with... the waves," Freya finished lamely, realising she almost told her secret! "And that's where I saw him last, helping Lisbet get into the boat."

They all stood silently, staring at the bleak sea. Small waves pushed towards the shore; a trickling, gurgling sound that seemed so gentle it was hard to imagine two people drowning in it. There was no sign of a havfrue's tail. Or a man floating. Freya turned to her father, feeling a sob collect in her throat.

"Where is he, Pappa?"

Pappa's eyes were dark and filled with unshed tears as he looked down at her.

"Lille venn..."

"There!" Shouted Jens. "On the rocks over there!" They all ran, scrabbling over rocks. Freya didn't know what Jens had seen, she just held on tight to Mamma's hand as Jens and Pappa leapt like athletes with amazing speed. When the women caught up with them Freya saw them leaning over something spread out over a large rock - a limp, dark haired body, fully clothed. They were already turning him over, lifting him quickly to the grass where the two medics got to work. Monika checked the pulse, Jens spread his fingers on Onkel Felix's chest, leaned over him and started pushing down rhythmically. A splutter, a groan was heard. Onkel Felix was rolled over onto his side where he vomited and began breathing on his own. Freya flung herself forward and kissed his wet cheek. She stroked his dark hair out of his eyes.

"Onkel Felix, Onkel Felix…" she whispered.

Something made her turn her gaze to the fjord. A dark head briefly rose from the depths, two large eyes double blinked slowly, then the face sank again. There was a flick of a tail followed by a small, white splash.

"Thank you, Lorelei," Freya whispered. "Thank you for bringing him back to us."

CHAPTER TWENTY NINE

Mamma sang as she cooked dinner that night. Tante Nina was coming home tomorrow. Onkel Felix was staying the night in the spare attic bedroom upstairs. Everyone was safe. As she climbed the stairs to Lisbet's room Freya heard the soothing tones of Pappa's deep voice. She hesitated outside the door, knowing he had brought up a cup of hot chocolate he had made himself for his eldest daughter. Lisbet's light voice had a whiney edge to it, pleading. Their conversation seemed private. Freya turned and walked down the stairs.

The whole house smelled absolutely scrumptious, for Mamma was making her special crumbed steaks with brown sauce, creamy mashed potato and grilled tomatoes with caramelised onion. Mamma stood at the stove shrouded in steam, humming to herself. Freya wrapped her arms around Mamma's waist and laid her head against her mother's body. She could feel the vibrations of Mamma's voice through her cheek.

"Mamma, can I help with dinner?" she asked.

"You can lay the table if you like, vennen min."

"Shall we use the red placemats that Tante Nina made?"

"Why not. Good idea." Mamma took the large pot off the stove and drained the scalding water into the sink, using the lid.

Pappa came downstairs.

"Want me to mash the potatoes, *min elskede*, (my love)?" He asked, circling his arms around her waist and kissing her neck.

Mamma giggled.

"Oh, you! Don't distract me. And yes, you can mash them. They're the pink ones from last year's crop. Should be coming up nice and fluffy."

"Mm…" Pappa commented. "I'm glad I bothered to fertilise them twice. Freya, the best cutlery I think." He smiled at her, his handsome face relaxed and happy, his golden-brown eyes warm with affection.

Freya went to the beautiful wooden dresser in the lounge room. Opening the two wide drawers was opening a treasure trove. All of Mamma's best things, many being wedding gifts, were stored here: silver napkin rings etched with images of elk in a snowy forest, soft, white, damask table cloths, fine-cut glassware dishes, silver cutlery and hand crocheted doilies, one of which had been made by Gamle Jenny's own hand. Freya ran a fingertip over the tiny stitches of a pale blue table cloth embroidered with white Hardanger stitch. She gathered up the silver cutlery and red placemats and returned to the kitchen.

"Do you think Lisbet will come down for dinner, Mamma?"

Mamma turned from the bench, a covered pot held between red oven mitts. She placed it in the centre of the table on a wooden trivet.

"I think she needs to rest, little one. She's had quite a shock and her body is very weak. But she'll be up and around again in a few days I expect. Would you like to fetch Onkel Felix? I think he's out of the shower now. The pipes have stopped rattling." She grinned.

Music drifted gently from the room where Onkel Felix was to sleep that night. Guitar, flute and a soft female voice. Freya knocked timidly on the partly open door.

"Come in," he called. As she entered Freya saw Onkel Felix sitting on the bed drying his wet hair with a towel. His chest was bare and he wore shorts, something she had rarely seen. A jagged surgical scar ran down the length of his left leg. It didn't matter how many times she saw it, Freya was always shocked at the savagery of the thick, reddened line, as if a giant had scrawled there just for fun. He saw her watching.

"It's not the prettiest thing in the world, is it?" He said with a rueful smile.

"Oh, no, it's fine. Sorry for staring at it," Freya replied.

"That's okay, Freya. It's a part of me. Has been for a long time."

"Does this mean you're not mad at Mamma anymore?" Freya blurted, then realised and swallowed nervously.

Onkel Felix puffed out a breath, the corner of his mouth lifted and Freya waited for the familiar sneer to return to his face. Instead, he stood and tossed the towel to a chair.

"I have realised that life is precious, Freya. Too precious to waste it feeling angry at someone for something they did by accident."

"Oh! That will make Mamma so happy!" Freya ran to hug him. "You're the best uncle in the world," she murmured.

His arms encircled her.

"And you are an amazing young lady - the way you drove the boat back to shore and got help for your sister."

They pulled apart from each other and shared a rare moment of smiles.

At dinner the adults were happy, toasting each other with glasses of cider. Mamma's cheeks grew quite rosy and her laughter a little louder than usual. Pappa and Onkel Felix slapped each other on the back several times, laughing at stories from their teenage years and teasing each other. Freya watched avidly, feeling so relieved and happy right down to her insides.

A scream from upstairs ripped through the air.

Pappa leapt from his chair with such force it tipped and clattered to the floor. Onkel Felix and Mamma were on their feet heading for the stairs, Freya behind. Pappa took the stairs two at a time and flung open Lisbet's door. She was sobbing and screaming by turns – the most horrifying sound Freya had ever heard.

"What is it, Lisbet?" Mamma cried as they entered the bedroom. Pappa was already sitting on the edge of the bed cradling Lisbet's head to his chest, stroking her hair.

"Sh… Sh my Lisbet. Sh my girl," he said softly.

Lisbet quietened. The rest of them stood watching silently. Waiting. Waiting for the explanation. Finally, Lisbet pulled free of her father and looked up at him with such anguish his face went completely white with shock. His big hand trembled as he reached out to touch her tangled hair. Hiccupping, Lisbet tried to speak.

"I…I fell asleep. And I had a nightmare," she said, so softly they could hardly hear her.

"Kjære Lisbet, what is it?" Mamma whispered, sitting on the bed and patting Lisbet's legs, smoothing the blanket over and over.

Lisbet took a big shaky breath, her blue eyes huge, her elegant brows drawn together.

"I have to tell you something."

Mamma leaned forward, her face pale.

"Do you want us all in here?"

"I can go," offered Onkel Felix, turning back towards the door.

Lisbet held up a hand.

"No, it's fine. I want to tell you all." She shook her head sadly. "I can't keep it inside any longer." She met her father's gaze. "Please don't be mad, Pappa!" She sobbed, squeezing his hand desperately.

"No, no, never!" he insisted gently. "In your own time. We'll wait. We're all here for you."

"Yes, Liebling," Mamma said softly, tears glistening in her dark blue eyes.

Lisbet's gaze fell.

"I feel so ashamed. It was my fault. I should never have gone there…"

"Where?" Pappa asked, searching her face.

Lisbet raised her eyes.

"To Ragnar's house."

Mamma frowned, confused.

"When did you do this, vennen min?"

"When I ran away. That's where I went. At first. He said I was so pretty. He said…" She started to cry.

Pappa and Mamma exchanged worried glances.

"What…" Pappa swallowed. "What happened?"

"He… said he had some really beautiful photos of the mountains and birds. Eagles." Lisbet shook her head angrily. "I was so stupid! I believed him! I didn't even listen to my intuition, you know? There was no one else home. We were alone, and…I had a bad feeling and I ignored it. Oh, Mamma!" She reached for her mother's arms. Pappa got up and went to stand next to his older brother. The men stood with arms folded and deep frowns on their faces.

"I'll call the police in the morning," Pappa said gravely.

Onkel Felix nodded.

"This has to be dealt with properly. To make sure it doesn't happen again." He flicked a glance at Freya, who was watching everyone, trying to figure out what they were talking about.

"What happened to Lisbet, Pappa?" she asked.

He crouched in front of her and held her thin shoulders in his big, work-worn hands.

"She was taken advantage of. I don't want to give you the details Freya. You're too young."

"But…"

"No," he said firmly, his eyes locked onto hers.

"This is big sister and adult stuff." He flicked a glance at Lisbet. "We all need you to accept this, Freya. And not tell anyone at school. Can you do that for me, lille venn?"

Freya nodded.

"I know you're disappointed. I know it doesn't make sense. One day perhaps Lisbet will tell you herself."

"But for now," added Mamma, "Lisbet needs all our love and understanding.

"I'm twelve now. I understand a lot, you know!" Freya insisted, feeling left out.

"Freya," Lisbet said, sniffing. "Come here." Freya sat on the bed. Lisbet took her hand and squeezed it. Her eyes were red and puffy. Her lips trembled. She was trying very hard to be brave. "Ragnar… did something mean to me. And now I'm embarrassed and ashamed. It's made me feel stupid because I should have seen it coming, but…" She paused and stroked Freya's hair, just like Mamma often did. Freya hung her head. This was Lisbet's secret. Too painful to share.

"You don't have to tell me. It will probably make you feel worse anyway."

"Thank you," Lisbet whispered and kissed Freya's forehead. "You're the best, most special sister in the world." She lifted Freya's chin so their eyes met. "And thank you for being so brave, so brave to rescue me like that!"

Freya kissed her sister's cheek. "I know you'd do the same for me." As she stood she saw that all the adults had tears in their eyes.

Even Onkel Felix.

CHAPTER THIRTY

Freya woke next morning feeling exhausted. Raising her heavy head she looked out the small attic window. Blue, blue sky greeted her. The world was happy again. Everything was right in her world. But Freya felt troubled. Something dreadful had happened to Lisbet and no one would tell her what it was. She couldn't quite accept that the adults kept a secret from her, that they thought her too young to understand. As she swung her legs over the edge of the bed Freya felt angry. They still treated her like a small child! Why didn't they realise she was older now, perfectly capable of understanding more complicated things. As she went to her mirror and picked up her hairbrush, Freya looked at her reflection and saw a girl with big brown eyes like her father and strong brows like her Onkel Felix. She took out the messy braid she had worn to keep her hair tidy in bed and brushed slowly, with deliberate strokes that matched her thoughts.

They don't trust me. They think I'm too silly. They think I'm too young.

But no matter how angry she felt, Freya knew in her heart that Lisbet had been through enough and that to insist to be told the secret would be selfish. With a sigh she put down her brush and picked up a hair elastic. Plaiting her chestnut brown hair into one long braid, the same as Mamma, Freya looked into her own eyes.

"You're not silly. You're smart and one day, soon, they will realise that you're not a little child anymore and you deserve to know things." Turning away from the mirror Freya dressed and went downstairs for breakfast.

Lisbet sat in her usual seat at the table, her hair neatly brushed, her face calm, her cheeks rosy. Relieved, Freya sat next to her.

"You look good this morning, Lisbet. Did you sleep okay?" Freya asked, picking up a knife and reaching out for a slice of warm toast from the rack.

"I feel pretty good," Lisbet said, turning to her little sister with a smile. "Thanks to you."

Freya wasn't used to compliments from her sister. She wasn't used to being smiled at even. Her gaze followed the others sitting at the table. Mamma poured tea from her favourite silver teapot which was dressed in a pink and white crocheted cover that made it look like a large, frilly tulip. Onkel Felix held out his cup and offered his sister-in-law a shy smile.

"Thank you, Gretchen," he said. "You always make the tea just right."

Mamma blushed. Freya giggled. She wasn't used

to the interaction between these two being so happy and harmonious. Pappa crunched on his toast noisily and slurped his tea.

"I reckon I did pretty well snagging this young girl," he said tweaking Mamma's cheek. She blushed again.

"Oh you! Still being a silly young pup, after all these years!"

"Puppy love," he said, giving her a knowing look.

"Oh, please!" Lisbet protested. "Enough of the smoochy stuff!"

They all laughed.

The door opened and in strode Onkel Stefan. Freya leapt to her feet and rushed towards him.

"Onkel Stefan! You missed all the excitement! Lisbet nearly drowned and Onkel Felix nearly drowned and..." She stopped short of mentioning Lorelei.

Onkel Stefan lifted Freya up into his arms. She wrapped her legs around his waist as if she were four or five years old.

"It seems I'm not the only child hero in this family," he said, laughing. Freya grinned, wrapped her arms around his neck and kissed his stubbled cheek.

"Good to see you are okay, brother," Onkel Stefan said to Onkel Felix. Without a word Onkel Felix got awkwardly to his feet and shuffled round until he was facing his youngest brother square-on. Then he drew him into a tight hug. Onkel Stefan patted his brother awkwardly, his eyes wide with surprise.

"Thank you for searching for me," Onkel Felix said quietly.

"Well I wasn't very successful!" Onkel Stefan said

with a chuckle, giving his brother a gentle slap on the back before seating himself and reaching for a plate of toast. He began buttering the golden toasted bread, then lavished it with thick slices of brun ost and topped this off with a big spoonful of Mamma's home-made strawberry jam. For a few seconds he couldn't speak, munching happily, rolling his eyes in delight. "How I missed your cooking, Gretchen! The food at the motel was quite disgusting."

Pappa grinned.

"See anyone there we know?" He said with a knowing look. Onkel Stefan shifted uncomfortably in his seat and rather than reply, shoved in another mouthful of toast. "Now that you've just arrived, we're about to leave for the first ferge," Pappa said.

"Oh?" Onkel Stefan slurped his tea appreciatively.

"We're going to fetch Nina from the hospital."

Onkel Stefan's teacup fell to the saucer with a clatter.

"Is she alright? What happened?" He looked around at all their faces.

Pappa held up his hand.

"She's fine. A false alarm." He looked at Freya a little nervously. "They just decided to keep her in overnight, to be sure, that's all. I suppose we could all go, if you like."

"That won't be necessary, Torstein," said Mamma. "I have so much to do here. And I don't think Lisbet is quite up to travelling yet."

"I think I'll just sit on the verandah for a while and read a book," Lisbet said quietly. "I'm sure Tante Nina won't mind."

"Of course," Pappa said. "I don't want to push you."

"And travelling on the ferge might not be pleasant for Lisbet right now," Onkel Felix said, meaningfully.

"Ah, yes." Pappa looked abashed.

"Can we talk about something else?" Lisbet said, redness rising up her neck and into her face."

"Sorry, Liebling. We really shouldn't talk about this in front of you. Or Freya," Mamma said. "How about we make something delicious for Tante Nina, Freya?"

Freya wordlessly held out her teacup for Mamma to refill. Slowly she stirred in some sugar and added a plop of milk. She wanted to say the right thing, to appear grown-up, not a petulant child wanting her way at the expense of other people's feelings.

"Okay Mamma," she said with a smile. "I'm just so glad Lisbet and Onkel Felix are safe. And soon Tante Nina will be home and the world will be perfect again."

"Well, I'll drink to that!" Onkel Felix said, holding aloft his teacup, his face beaming.

"Me too!" Onkel Stefan added, raising his teacup as well. They all chinked them together gently.

"So, did you run into anyone interesting on the mainland?" Pappa tried again. Onkel Stefan blushed. "I see!" Pappa tipped back his head and laughed. "Good to see that some things never change, little brother."

CHAPTER THIRTY ONE

Later that morning, after she'd fed the chickens and tidied her room, Freya took some sweet biscuits from the cookie jar and put them in her pocket. As she stood on the gently sloping lawn outside the kitchen, and looked up to the trees behind Fjellheim, she saw movement in the shadows. Standing perfectly still, she breathed in the sharp, green scent of spring and waited. But whatever it was, it made no move. Freya gave in and walked off down the slope towards the shore. She had more important things to do today.

Settling herself on her favourite rock she began to sing, hoping to call Lorelei to the shore. She had seen a frightening side to her friend and wasn't entirely sure she could trust the havfrue, but then, Lorelei had brought Onkel Felix back to them. In all probability had saved his life. And Freya felt she ought to thank her.

But the maiden of the deep was reluctant to show herself today, despite the sunshine sparkling off the water and the cool breeze ruffling Freya's hair gently, carrying the tangy smell of the sea as well as the sweet apple blossom from Gamle Jenny's small orchard. Freya scanned the fjord waters, spread out smoothly like glass today. On the other side of the fjord, a speedboat sped across in front of the township of Stranda, its white wake visible as it headed up the fjord. All the snow which had fallen on Bollen had now melted and the troll sat in his bath as before, without his white cap. Freya took off her shoes and socks and paddled in the cold water, wriggling her toes over the slippery yellow seaweed, gripping the smooth grey striped rocks. She bent to pick up a tiny shell nestled in the sand. It wasn't nearly as special as the shell Lorelei had brought her. There was no intricate pattern, just dull, purple and black colouring. Nevertheless, Freya put it in her other pocket as a keepsake. Then she remembered the cookies and decided to eat one. Settling on a rock once more she nibbled at the edges round and round, then nibbled the next round until there was just a small piece left which she held on her tongue until it melted. Scanning the water once more she hoped with all her heart that Lorelei would come, but it seemed not to be. Disappointed, she got up, collected her shoes and socks and began to walk up the slope.

A sharp bark made her stop and turn. Lorelei sat on her usual rock, calmly regarding Freya with her large, serene, alien eyes.

"Lorelei!" Freya cried, rushing back down to the shore. "I knew you'd come. I want to thank you for saving Onkel Felix's life yesterday. Here." She held out the two cookies. Lorelei tilted her head first one side then the other, eyeing the baked goods on Freya's small hand. Then she reached out and took them, rubbing one of them on her arm until it disintegrated into a crumbly mess.

"No, no!" Freya giggled. She mimicked putting the cookie in her mouth. "You eat it. Like this."

Lorelei chittered, her pointed chin quivering. And then, to Freya's amazement, she put the entire biscuit into her narrow mouth and crunched on it with her pointy teeth. Freya watched, feeling certain Lorelei would spit it out at any moment. But the havfrue swallowed and looked at Freya expectantly, holding out her hand for more.

"Sorry, no more. I only brought three and because I thought you weren't coming I ate one myself," Freya admitted sheepishly. "But I'm so glad you liked it! Tomorrow I'll bring you some more."

Lorelei reached out to Freya and made a soft whining noise in her throat.

"What is it?" Freya said. "What is it Lorelei? Are you hurt? Is something wrong?"

Lorelei made the soft keening sound again, reaching for Freya. Freya stepped closer, wary, the incidents of yesterday sharp in her mind. She heard Gamle Jenny's voice saying, *the sea has a soul, but no compassion.* Standing just at the edge of Lorelei's grasp, she took the havfrue's hand in hers. Lorelei allowed her to turn the hand over this way and that, to study the speckled, grey-green skin, to run her thumb over the softly smooth surface.

"Your skin is beautiful," Freya whispered. "Just like human skin." She looked into Lorelei strange eyes and sensed the wild heart beating in the havfrue's chest. "But you're not human, are you? You're special. You're wild. And I expected too much from you."

Lorelei tilted her head and studied Freya's face earnestly. Whining, she reached up with her long fingers to touch the side of Freya's face. Then she patted her own bare muscular chest and grunted.

"I'm not sure what you're saying," Freya said. "But I know I cannot come with you, down into the deep of the fjord, where you live. Is that what you were trying to do for Lisbet yesterday? Take her down to where you live? Perhaps you thought you were doing the right thing. Perhaps you thought you were saving her." Freya shook her head. "I don't know. I probably will never know the truth." She looked into Lorelei's eyes. "But I don't think I can fully trust you." She squeezed Lorelei's hand and patted the back of it gently. "I just have to accept that you're a wild creature and feel so, so lucky to have you as my friend." She smiled at Lorelei.

Lorelei's mouth twitched. She lifted the corners with her long fingers.

Freya laughed. "That's it! That's an almost-smile."

Lorelei chittered and pointed to the fjord, slapped her own chest and pointed to Freya and then at the fjord again.

"I know," Freya said softly. "You want me to come. And I'm sure it's lovely down there. But my home is here." She pointed at her beautiful old wooden house sitting on the hill, where it had for a hundred years. "That's my home. And my family are there too. And I need them." Sadness overwhelmed Freya and she brushed tears from her eyes.

Lorelei reached out and gently touched the corners of Freya's eye with a fingertip. She whined.

"Tears. I'm sad." Freya nodded.

Lorelei made an odd sound, something like a hiccup, the tips of her little pointed teeth showing, her mouth open in a grimace. Freya heard the pain in that sound. The longing.

"This is goodbye, isn't it?" She said softly.

Lorelei barked suddenly. Then turned and in a flash, had slid gracefully back into the sea. All that was left was a splash and the flick of a frilly tail.

"Goodbye," Freya whispered. "And thank you for being my friend."

Freya trudged slowly back up to Fjellheim feeling like she had achieved and lost something significant both at the same time. Never had she heard of anyone having a havfrue as a friend. Never had anyone fought with a havfrue to rescue a human from their grasp. It seemed that the Askvold family had had their share of excitement, that was for sure.

A silver car was parked near the house, near the chicken coop and pen. Puzzled, Freya walked slowly to the back door. Tiny birds flitted in the trees, their excited squeaks capturing Freya's attention. The fledgling! She stood stock still, waiting to see what would happen. The parents flew in and out anxiously. And then a fluff ball appeared at the edge of the nest, high up in the tree. A light breeze ruffled the leaves. The fledgling suddenly fell. With a cry of horror, Freya lurched forward. It sat fluttering on the grass below. Gently, she gathered it into her hands where it wriggled, terrified at this giant who had captured it.

"It's okay," she whispered to it. Its tiny black eyes spied her. Its tiny little beak opened with a squeak. It struggled to open its wings and pushed with its teensy little legs against the confines of her hand.

"Oh, all right then," Freya said, opening her hands. The fledgling sat on her open palm, its little head tilting from side to side. With her back to the breeze, Freya suddenly lifted her hands up into the air and the fledgling launched itself. It's clumsy, bumbling flight took it to a nearby May bush wear it crash landed, cheeping loudly. Its parents immediately flew to it, their excited cries making Freya smile.

As she opened the door to the kitchen, Freya was greeted with delight.

"Freya! Come here my brave girl!" Pappa said warmly.

Seated at the kitchen table was a strange man, a notebook and pen in front of him on the table. He stood and reached out his hand.

"So this is young Freya? My name is Markus and I'm here to interview you for my newspaper."

"Interview?" Freya shrank back against Pappa. "What for?"

Markus smiled broadly and tapped his notepad with his pen.

"This is an amazing story, young lady. And the people of this area would love to know about it."

In her mind, Freya saw disturbing images of fishermen with nets trying to capture Lorelei, dragging her screaming from the deep, her pointy teeth gnashing together, her eyes wild with fear and loathing. Freya face felt hot and her chest heaved.

"What's wrong, lille venn?" Said Mamma, feeling Freya's forehead with a warm hand. "Are you ill, Liebling?"

Freya shook her head. How could they do this to Lorelei? How could they tell her secret? It was the worst betrayal Freya could think of.

"I don't want to be interviewed!" She blurted and turned on her heel and ran up the stairs before anyone could stop her.

CHAPTER THIRTY TWO

There was a knock on Freya's door. Pappa's voice came through the wood.

"Freya? May I come in?"

"Yes, all right." Freya turned over on her bed from where she had buried her face in the pillow, crying softly for the loss of Lorelei. Pappa came in and sat on the edge of Freya's bed. Taking her small hand in his he squeezed it gently.

"I know this is hard for you. Some very dramatic, near death experiences in just a couple of days. It's a lot to take in. And of course you're concerned about your secret."

Freya looked at him, wide eyed.

"So you believe in Lorelei?"

Pappa smiled broadly.

"You believed in her when no one else did. And my brother fought with her to save my daughter. How can I not believe?"

"Onkel Felix told you?" Fear crept up Freya's spine. "But I don't want them to find her! I don't want them down here with their cameras and newspaper people trying to catch her in their nets! They'd hurt her and take her off to a museum!"

"Sh. Freya. That's not going to happen. I do understand it's a precious secret that you want to keep just within our family and so you should." He squeezed her hand. "But there's another side to this story, Freya. You did something truly amazing for a girl your age. And Mamma and I are *so proud* of you." He pulled her in for a hug. As she leaned against her father's chest and heard the slow rhythmic drum of his heart Freya knew she could trust him. Lorelei could trust him. She pulled away and looked into his eyes.

"So, they want to interview me, but they won't be told anything about Lorelei?"

He nodded.

"Well, I suppose I could tell them what happened," Freya said. She looked out the window at the blue sky and her mind went back to that moment where Lorelei surfaced clutching her sister and then sank to the depths again. She shivered. "She belongs in the fjord, in the deep. Where she's been for such a long time. She's a wild creature. I don't want anyone knowing about her." She looked at her father "Will you promise? And Onkel Felix too? No one will know?"

"Not even Onkel Stefan, if that's what you want."

Freya considered for a moment.

"Well I guess it can't hurt to tell him," she said. "He is family. And I'm sure if I explain it he will understand how important it is to keep it a secret."

"I'm sure he will."

"So is that man still here? Markus?"

Pappa nodded.

"I told him I would see how you felt about telling your story. We've already told him the little that we know. And he's going to visit Gamle Jenny to find out her version as well."

Freya swung her legs over the edge of the bed and stood.

"Well I'd better make sure he gets the right story then."

Pappa smiled and followed her downstairs.

Two days later a parcel arrived at the post office for the Askvold family. Freya rode on her bike to get it. The Eikeberg post office was in a small, wooden building of about two hundred years old, situated on the top of the hill, near the school. Freya rode home as fast as she could, her feet pedalling so quickly they were a blur and the chain ticking so fast it hummed as she rode down from the top of the hill towards the turnoff to Askvold dairy. She saw old Mrs Vestad walking along to the bus stop. They waved at each other as Freya indicated left and turned up the long driveway. Down through the pine trees she free wheeled, the soft needles making a crackling sound under her tyres, past Gamle Jenny's house standing bright in the sunshine. Then she pedalled fast again along the path to Fjellheim. Dropping the bicycle near the back door she raced inside, puffing with excitement and exertion.

"The parcel! Here's the parcel!" She handed it to Mamma and they all gathered round to look, leaving their cups of tea and slices of cake on the table. It contained five copies of the local newspaper and on the front page was a very nice photo, a close-up, of Freya with the fjord in the background. There were smaller photos of Bestefar's boat and a shot of Lisbet taken from a distance, sitting at the shoreline, staring out to the fjord. It was the only photo she would allow them to take of her.

Mamma held the newspaper at arm's length, a broad smile on her face.

"Look at this! Look at this beautiful photo of our Freya! And what a wonderful story he is telling, that reporter. He did a good job."

"You look lovely, Freya," exclaimed Tante Nina, smiling, taking the newspaper Mamma offered her. "Look at those big beautiful brown eyes. Just like your Pappa."

"Yes," commented Onkel Felix, his arm gently held around his wife's waist as he looked over her shoulder.

Pappa kissed Mamma's cheek and smiled.

"Look at that brave young girl. Our young girl."

Onkel Stefan shook his copy and read the article with a serious look on his face.

"Well, I'm pleased to see they didn't mention Lorelei at all."

"Yes," Mamma said gravely. "Gamle Jenny didn't mention it either, which is good because I forgot to run over and warn her."

Freya was reminded of the saying Gamle Jenny

had told her: *the sea has a soul, but no compassion.* She regarded the photo of herself.

"Well, I guess it's an okay photo of me," she commented.

Lisbet was quietly looking at the photo of herself, down by the water.

"I look lonely," she said. There was silence as everyone turned to look at her. There was worry in Mamma's face. Freya patted her sister's arm.

"I think you look mysterious and cool," she said with admiration. "Like a model in a painting."

Lisbet smiled at her sister. "Yeah, I guess so."

Onkel Stefan said, "Well, I think you both look adorable. But I could be biased." He grinned and drew them both in for a hug. And for once, Lisbet didn't pull away or grimace. She smiled up at her uncle, her face shining with happiness.

CHAPTER THIRTY THREE

The next week Lisbet returned to school. As they left the house, walked up through the pine trees to the bus shelter, Freya tried to think of happy things to talk about. She pointed out the way the sunlight sparkled on the fjord that day, the cries of seagulls as they flew overhead, the little white daisies popping up along the verge. Lisbet half smiled and murmured replies, but Freya could see her sister was deeply worried about how the other teenagers would react to her return. Would they somehow know what had happened? Lisbet had taken great care to braid her hair in an unusual style, which suited her beautiful skin, sweet smile and pale blue eyes. She wore her best jeans, a soft white top and new sneakers. Making a good impression was important to Lisbet.

Their shoes crunched on the gravel as they

approached the old milk churn shed and sat down on the wooden bench. Freya watched the fluffy white clouds passing in the pale blue sky. She had run out of positive things to say, sensing Lisbet just wanted to be alone with her thoughts. The minibus came up the road towards them. They boarded, and instead of sitting up the front by herself, Lisbet took Freya's hand and made her way to the back seat where they sat together. Freya felt the need to pat her sister on the back, to reassure her. But suddenly Lisbet's face clouded over. She wrenched out the hair elastic and started to undo her braid.

"But it looked so pretty!" Freya exclaimed.

"I don't want to look different," Lisbet replied quietly. "I don't want people to notice me at all."

"Oh. Well, you look like you usually do. Still pretty though."

"Thanks." Lisbet looked into her sister's eyes. "You did nothing wrong, you know. It's not your fault at all, Freya. So, I'm sorry if I'm grumpy. But this is... a difficult day for me. I don't know what's going to happen or how people are going to react."

Freya thought about it for a second.

"They'll just think you're being your dramatic self," she said with an impish grin.

"Har, har," Lisbet said, smiling.

As they walked through the school gates Lisbet's friends rushed towards her, not with concern, as she had feared, but with happy smiles and greetings. Freya turned to find her own friends. She made her way towards Britt, who was sitting on the bench underneath cherry tree.

It was a beautiful spring day, all day. The sun was warm on the playground and the children ran around like mad things, their faces shining, their cheeks rosy.

Later that afternoon, as they walked past Gamle Jenny's house, Freya took in deep breaths of the fresh air, scanning the water for signs of Lorelei but knowing in her heart she probably would never see her again. She thought she saw a tiny splash out in the middle, perhaps the flick of a frilly tail. But it didn't matter. Freya's secret was precious, something she would hold inside her heart forever, whether she saw her friend again or not. Lorelei had chosen her. And nothing could take that honour away.

As they opened the kitchen door they were met with the smell of vanilla cookies baking in the oven and the excited cries of their mother, who stood hugging Onkel Felix. Lisbet and Freya looked at each other, puzzled.

"Hei *jentene*, (girls)," Mamma said, her face beaming. "Onkel Felix is about to leave for the hospital. He is going to be a father today! Isn't that the most wonderful news?"

Freya looked quickly at her sister, remembering the look of terror on her face when Tante Nina had mentioned she was pregnant. But to her credit, Lisbet wasn't fazed. She approached her uncle, arms wide and a smile on her face.

"Congratulations, Onkel Felix," she said, giving him a hug.

Freya rushed in and joined in the hug.

"Yes! It's so exciting! I hope it's a boy." She could feel her uncle's strong arms around her and it made her feel safe and secure. Something she had never really associated with him before. There was a warmth about the man that was so new that she was still getting used to it. His dark eyes sparkled with mirth. The lines of pain on his face had seemed to have vanished. He was a handsome young man awaiting the birth of his first child, like any other husband.

"Now," Mamma said. "You must let him go. He doesn't want to miss anything."

"Um, I don't mean to be, um, I hope this isn't the wrong thing to say but isn't it a bit early?" Lisbet said, looking anxiously at Mamma.

Mamma dried her hands on her floral apron. She cast a glance at Onkel Felix.

"Yes," she nodded. "It is a little early. But all will be well. You just wait and see. This child is going to be born into a family of love."

As he nodded, Onkel Felix had tears in his eyes.

"No better family to be born into, I reckon."

Mamma shooed him out the door.

"Now, off you go! Don't miss this moment. She needs you there."

Pappa and Onkel Stefan came in from the milking later that afternoon, stamping their feet, the earthy smell of milk, cows and dung clinging to their clothes, their cheeks reddened from the wind. Freya and Lisbet were doing their homework at the kitchen table. Pappa went straight to the kettle to make coffee.

"So, Freya, isn't this exciting?" He said, spooning in the coffee and pouring some water. Mamma handed him the milk. He passed the cup to his younger brother and then made another.

"I still can't believe grumpy old Felix is going to be a dad," Onkel Stefan said jokingly.

"He'll make a wonderful dad!" Freya exclaimed in her uncle's defence, remembering how he had hauled her into his boat and encased her in his warm jumper.

Onkel Stefan's eyes crinkled with laughter.

"Of course he will." He leaned back in his chair and sipped his coffee. "And I will be the favourite uncle."

Lisbet snorted, but kept her head down as she finished her maths homework.

"You doubt this, young lady? You doubt the power of the youngest, most handsome uncle in this family?"

Lisbet looked up at him and tried to maintain a look of disdain but broke out into giggles.

"Let's hope the baby doesn't learn all your bad habits," she commented, turning the page and beginning at the top of the next. She consulted her textbook and kept writing. Onkel Stefan grinned but didn't reply.

At bedtime Freya wanted to know if there were any updates from the hospital.

"Now Freya, you need to go up to bed," Mamma said. "As soon as we know anything, we will tell you."

"Even if it's in the middle of the night?" Freya asked hopefully.

For a moment Mamma hesitated, but then seeing the earnest look on her youngest daughter's face, she caved in.

"Yes."

"Promise?"

"Of course. Now go to bed!" Mamma took Freya's face between her hands and kissed each cheek.

"Night, Pappa." Freya hugged him, but hesitated at the foot of the stairs. Her sister walked past, grabbed her hand and pulled her.

"Come on! The sooner you get to sleep, the sooner you will hear the news."

"That never works!" Freya grumbled, but followed.

Freya dreamed of Lorelei that night, of flying through the water, her long hair streaming behind her, holding hands with the havfrue, seeing wonders she never thought possible. And the best part was that she could breathe underwater. Lorelei showed her a cave at the bottom of the fjord, filled with treasures. As her eyes adjusted to the murky light, Freya was able to see everything clearly. Just as Lorelei was offering Freya something to eat, something squirming and alive, Freya was woken by her mother's gentle shaking of her arm.

"Freya, wake up Liebling."

"What? What is it? Is it the baby?"

Mamma sat on the edge of the bed and switched on the bedside table lamp. She caressed the side of Freya's face.

"You have a new cousin, Freya."

"A girl? A boy?"

"A boy." Mamma was beaming. "The first Askvold son of this generation."

Freya flung her arms around her mother's neck. "What are they going to call him?"

"Jan Petter," Mamma said.

"Petter, after Bestefar?"

Mamma nodded.

"Jan is Tante Nina's father's name."

"It's a great name," Freya said. "Jan Petter. I like it."

Mamma chuckled. "I'm so glad. I'll make sure to tell them that you approve." Freya giggled and hugged her mother again.

"This is the best news in ages! Wait until I tell Britt tomorrow."

CHAPTER THIRTY FOUR

As Freya walked into the playground the next morning she noticed Britt wasn't sitting on their usual bench under the cherry tree, the ground covered in a thick, soft blanket of pale pink blossom. Another girl sat there, a new girl, in a bright blue jumper and jeans, with blue and red striped socks in her sneakers and her brown hair braided neatly in two plaits.

Freya approached the new girl. She sat, not too close.

"Hei. I'm Freya. You're new, aren't you?"

The girl turned to Freya. She had a heart shaped face and her nose was slightly turned up at the end which reminded Freya of a pixie. Freya liked her straightaway.

"I'm Lise. I just moved here from Oslo," said the girl, pulling out a sandwich and biting into it.

"I live on Eikeberg," Freya replied, watching her,

SECRETS OF THE WATER MEADOW

wondering why she was eating lunch already.

"Where's that?" Lise asked.

"It's an island. I have to take a minibus and ferge just to get here."

"Every single day?"

Freya nodded. "It's not so bad." Freya picked up a twig and started breaking it into pieces. "I really like being on the ferge. The water is sparkly and beautiful. Especially on a day like today."

"You're not scared of the water?"

"No, not really," Freya said, pushing aside the memory of the day she almost drowned.

"Your parents let you swim on your own? Without supervision?" Lise asked, stuffing the last of the sandwich into her mouth and brushing crumbs off her lap.

"Well, no. But I do spend a lot of time down at the shore," Freya answered vaguely, remembering Lorelei with a twinge of sadness, but also a deep sense of privilege and pride.

Lise looked at Freya intently. She tilted her head on the side and studied Freya's face, weighing up a decision.

"Can I ask you something?"

"Sure. Anything." Freya settled her hands in her lap and waited.

"You promise you won't laugh?"

"Of course! Promise."

Lise leaned forward, her eyes sparkling.

"Do you believe in havfruer?"

PRONOUNCIATIONS
For *Secrets of the Water Meadow*

('r' sounds are rolled, unless indicated by *)

Eikeberg	ache-eh-bae-rg
Havfrue	halve-frew-eh
Stranda	strun-nuh
Fjell	f-yell
Heim	haym
Mørke	murk-eh
Engler	eng-leh-r
Lille	lil-leh
Venn	ven
Ferge	fae-r-geh
Blåfugl	blaw-foo-l
Blomster	blom-steh-r
Øyboer	er-ee-boo-er
Gamle	gum-leh
Jenny	yenny
Norsk	nosh-k
Syttende	soot-nn-deh
Mai	my
Håkon	hawk-on

Herdebrei	haer-deh-bray
Reven	reh-ven
Laks	lucks
Bløtkake	blurt-kah-keh (don't say the 'r')
Alle	ull-eh (as in gull)
Fugler	foo-leh-r
Ingangen	in-gung-en
Tyttebær	titteh-bae-r
Rosemaling	roos-eh-mah-ling
Brus	bruce
Fjøset	f-yur-set (don't say the 'r')
Kransekake	krun-seh-kah-keh
Bunad	boo-nahd
Knuppen	knoop-pen
Kjære	shae-reh
Deg	day
Skole	skoo-leh
Festen	festn
Lefse	lef-seh
Snuppen	snoop-pen
Havørn	halve-urn*
Ha det	ha-deh
Tusen takk	too-sen tuck
Min Elskede	min el-skeh-deh
Ragnar	rung-nar
Jan	Yahn

ABOUT THE AUTHOR

Dawn Meredith grew up in England, Australia and Norway. She lived in an old, white wooden house on an island in Norway with her sister and family. This story is fictional, but influenced by her experiences on the island, as an Australian girl surrounded by Norwegian family life. Dawn has authored fourteen books for children and young adults. She lives with her family on a hundred acre farm on the island of Tasmania, off the coast of Australia. She is also an Artist of very finely detailed watercolour pencil drawings of birds and marine life.

You can find her books online here:
www.dawnmeredithauthorlblogspot.com
and her artwork here:
https://www.redbubble.com/people/DingbatDesigns/shop